Peril

at PIER NINE

Peril
at PIER NINE

Penny Draper

COTEAU
BOOKS
FOR KIDS

Edited by Barbara Sapergia.
Cover photo: "Picked Strawberries: A schoolboy from Wigan proudly displays a crate of strawberries he has picked," detail. Fox Photos / Hulton Archive / Getty Images
Cover painting by Aries Cheung.
Cover design by Duncan Campbell.
Book design by Karen Steadman.
Printed and bound in Canada by Friesens.

Library and Archives Canada Cataloguing in Publication

Library and Archives Canada Cataloguing in Publication

Draper, Penny, 1957-
        Peril at pier nine / Penny Draper.

ISBN 978-1-55050-376-0
        I. Title.

PS8607.R36P47 2007   JC813'.6   C2007-904326-7

10 9 8 7 6 5 4 3 2 1

2517 Victoria Ave.   *Available in Canada & the US from*
Regina, Saskatchewan   Fitzhenry & Whiteside
Canada   S4P 0T2   195 Allstate Parkway
                                      Markham, ON,   L3R 4T8

The publisher gratefully acknowledges the financial support of its publishing program by: the Saskatchewan Arts Board, the Canada Council for the Arts, the Government of Canada through the Book Publishing Industry Development Program (BPIDP), Association for the Export of Canadian Books and the City of Regina Arts Commission.

To my father
John Douglas Clapp
who taught me to sail
from the shores of Ward's Island

CONTENTS

PROLOGUE

SHE WAS CALLED THE QUEEN. SHE WASN'T THE *sleekest of boats, but her sheer size put her into a class of her own. She was stately, that was the word. She was the S.S. Noronic, Queen of the Inland Seas, largest passenger steamer on the Great Lakes.*

Launched in 1913 during the worst November gale ever recorded, she was top-heavy and too skinny and had to be loaded with pig iron to stop her from tipping over. Her engines were all in the stern, giving her a fat rear end. These were not the characteristics of a lady. In fact, the Noronic's *appearance was so odd she earned a mention in* Ripley's Believe It or Not.

Some said she carried good luck in her hold. Others said she was cursed.

Either way, there was no doubt that she was special. Passengers enjoyed the finest foods, the most exciting entertainment and the loveliest staterooms. Even her steam whistle was famous.

For thirty-six years, the Noronic carried passengers between Canada and the United States. She brought luck to all who knew her. For some, like Jack Gordon and Henry Addison, meeting her would change their lives.

CHAPTER 1
Camp-out on Snake Island
Toronto Islands, Summer, 1949
Tuesday

"TELL US AGAIN, CAPTAIN CLAPP," PLEADED JACK. "Jack, you know this story by heart!" laughed the Captain. Before he retired to his little cottage on Ward's Island, which is part of the Toronto Islands, Captain Clapp had commanded some of the largest and most famous ships that plied the Great Lakes. He had a great mane of white hair and an even greater belly; both were shaking with amusement. The island boys were camping out on Snake Island and had invited the Captain to the campfire because he knew more stories than anybody. And he loved to talk.

"Aw, come on, Cap'n," called the boys. "We want to hear!"

Captain Clapp took his pipe out of his mouth and slowly, methodically, set about tamping and lighting it.

He smoked his pipe constantly, so his mouth looked funny without it. There was a deep groove in his lip where the pipe ought to be. The boys settled in as the Captain finished the job.

"You know we didn't used to live on an island, don't you?" he began. "All these bits of sand that make up the Toronto Islands were once attached to Toronto proper. Then in 1858 a mighty storm blew up and washed away one end. Our end, the end we call Ward's Island. Before that, you could walk right across to the city without getting your feet wet. After the storm, they built those cement breakwaters along both sides of the gap to stop the lake from taking any more of the land, and the Toronto Islands were born, separated from the mainland by the Eastern Gap." The boys all nodded. They knew that.

"Four years later, there was another terrible storm. Young William Ward, just fifteen years old… How old are you boys now?" the Captain asked.

"We're fourteen, Captain," Jack answered for the crew. Jack was the leader of the island boys. He always did all the talking. Blond, lanky and a bit of a rascal, Jack was well-known by everybody on Ward's Island. All the cottagers were happy to see him come and just as happy to see him go. It took a lot of energy to be around Jack.

"Well, he was just a little older than you. He decided to take his five younger sisters out for a bit of a sail."

"That was nice of him," said Beans, who was eating watermelon.

"Well, maybe," said the Captain slowly. "But the day was gusty. His father thought there might be a storm brewing. William went anyway; he was a fine sailor, just like our Jack here."

Jack sat up straighter and grinned broadly. Everybody knew he was the best sailor on the island.

"And just like Jack, he didn't think before he acted."

Jack slumped back down.

"William took the girls out and they had a fine time. Then William turned about and headed for home. All of a sudden the wind caught the sail and knocked William overboard. The boat capsized, throwing the girls into the water. They all grabbed onto William. He struggled to right the boat and got three of the girls into it. The fourth sister climbed in to the boat by herself. The fifth hung onto the side."

"Then what happened?" asked the boys, who already knew but loved the way the Captain told the story.

"Another gust caught the sail. The boat capsized again. Three girls were lost to the lake. The fourth sister disappeared. The fifth hung on as long as she could. William struggled to get to her. But in the end all the girls were lost. All five."

"After that, young William was nearly undone. He dedicated himself to rescuing those in peril at sea."

There was quiet around the campfire.

Then Jack piped up. "Tell us about the *Jane Ann Marsh*, Captain Clapp."

"It was December, six years later. The schooner *Jane Ann Marsh* was wrecked just outside the Eastern Gap in a blinding snowstorm. None of the islanders even knew. The blizzard was so intense that they couldn't see the mast through the snow. The first anybody knew about it was the next morning when some of her cargo washed up on shore."

"William and his friend Robert got into a skiff. The islanders tied lifelines on them and pushed them out into the storm. As they rowed out to the wreck, the skiff upset three times. Each time the lifelines saved them. When they finally got to the *Jane Ann,* William and Robert tied up to the wreck. They found the crew clinging to the mast, where they had climbed to stay out of the water as the boat slowly sank. But up high and exposed to the blizzard, the crew of the *Jane Ann* had frozen to the mast. The men were too numb to move by themselves, but they were still alive. William and Robert each took a piece of cordwood and pounded the ice off the crew."

"The skiff would only take two to shore at a time. Each time the skiff returned to the shore, the island women took charge of the rescued sailors. The island men broke the ice off the skiff, readying it for its next trip. While they did that, William and Robert ran around in the snow to get their circulation going again. The rescue took seven hours. But every man was saved."

The Captain was pensive. He always got that way when he talked about disasters at sea. "In his lifetime, William Ward saved a hundred and sixty-four people from the waters of Toronto Harbour. They named this island after him. But none of that could bring back his five little sisters."

CHAPTER 2
Jack's Dream

THE CAMPFIRE WAS DYING DOWN TO EMBERS. The Captain heaved himself up off the log he'd been sitting on. "It's bedtime for me. I'm going back to my nice soft bed; enjoy the hard ground, boys!" The crew thanked the Captain for his stories, and set about unrolling the sleeping bags. Jack walked Captain Clapp out to the bridge that connected Snake Island to the rest of the Toronto Islands. Jack, as usual, had more questions.

"Have you ever rescued anybody, Captain?" asked Jack.

"I was a laker captain for forty years, Jack, what do you think?" replied the Captain. "There're two things you got to worry about at sea: storms and fire. Both hit right out of the blue; you never know they're coming.

And when they hit, the captain is responsible for what happens. You can't run, and you can't panic. The lives of your crew and your passengers depend on you. I know all you boys are good sailors. You're comfortable in the water, and that's good. But don't ever disrespect the lake. It's bigger and stronger than you'll ever be."

The pair walked companionably together. "You sure love those stories, Jack. I've never seen another like you," said the Captain.

"My mom says I was born for the sea," replied Jack. "I'm going to be a laker captain just like you. I know I can do it. I'm a good sailor; I know the wind and the waves. And the other kids listen to me. They're going to be my crew."

"You're right, Jack, the other kids listen to you," Captain Clapp replied seriously. "And that's a problem. A captain can't act without thinking, and you do. You're more likely to lead your friends into danger than out of it. You've got guts, but you have some growing up to do. Don't be talking to me about being a captain until you do."

The Captain strode away into the night. Jack felt a flush of anger. The Captain was old; he didn't know what he was talking about. Jack would never lead his crew into trouble. How could he? Nothing even remotely dangerous ever happened on the island.

Not that Ward's Island wasn't a great place to live. It was only ten minutes by ferry from the city of Toronto, where all the island dads worked. Most of the families moved into their summer cottages on the May long weekend and stayed until Thanksgiving; some even stayed all winter. The same kids came back every year and everybody felt like family. There were lots of things to do, like baseball and swimming and especially sailing, which was Jack's favourite. There was an island constable, but nothing bad ever happened, so the kids were allowed to stay up late and go anywhere they wanted. Jack and his crew could hop on their bikes early each morning and stay out until way after dark, and that was swell.

But danger? Jack wished it were possible. Then he could prove himself to the Captain. But the worst that could happen on Ward's Island was a flooded sidewalk or a stray baseball that bonked somebody on the head. William Ward had had plenty of opportunities to be a hero; Jack had none.

But he had to do something. The Great Lakes were in his blood, Jack felt it. He *would* follow in the Captain's footsteps; he *would* be a laker captain some day. Jack had even decided what boat he would captain. He reached into his pocket and pulled out a carefully folded advertisement.

ON THE "NORONIC" FOR A WEEK —
TOGETHER FAR OFF PORTS WE SEEK
Come Sail with Us for a Wonderful Week
Over the Glorious Inland Seas

Jack had a cigar box full of advertisements and pages ripped from *The Shipping News* under his bed and he spent hours studying the great ships, the freighters and the passenger cruisers. Gross tonnage, nautical speed, engine capacity and crew; he memorized every detail. By flashlight in his room, late at night, Jack had compared all the statistics and picked his ship. The *S.S. Noronic.*

She was the biggest passenger steamship on the Great Lakes, and the best; the flagship of the Canada Steamship Lines. She was the trickiest to manoeuvre, and the most respected in nautical circles. They called her the Queen of the Inland Seas. And she would be his.

All he had to do was prove to the Captain that he could handle it. Then the Captain would help him get a position on a training ship and he would be on his way.

But could he convince the Captain?

Jack clenched his fists with frustration. Then he walked back to the campfire and joined the other boys.

CHAPTER 3
Jack's Plan
Wednesday

"BYE, MOM!" JACK BANGED THE SCREEN DOOR on his way out. "Ferry's here." After vaulting the small fence in front of the cottage, Jack cocked his head and listened with a practiced ear. The low whistle of the *Sam McBride* sounded, and Jack pinpointed its location perfectly. He knew his boats. The ferry was closer than he had thought; he was late. He hopped on his bike and headed off at a dead tear.

Jack pedalled vigorously with his right foot. There were hundreds of bikes on the island because no cars were allowed, but Jack's bike was special. Known to everybody as "Jack's trusty steed," his bike had only one pedal, half a handlebar and no seat. Great skill was required to ride it. Jack was an expert, admired by all.

Sprinting down Channel Avenue, Jack pumped hard. The *Sam McBride* was already docked. Day picnickers were pouring off the boat. Holding his left foot out for balance, Jack careened around the corner of the Wiman Building then ran smack dab into the Van Camp's pushcart. The Van Camp's owned the biggest pushcart and everybody liked to borrow it when they had to move lots of gear. Today it was loaded with boxes.

Flying over the handlebar, Jack skidded across the boxes and somersaulted onto the ground. He sat up and blinked the dust out of his eyes as several picnickers rushed to help him.

"Are you all right, young man?" asked a woman anxiously.

"Oh, I do this all the time," grinned Jack. "I hope my bike's not hurt, though."

They all looked at Jack's bike. A girl with dark, curly hair started to laugh. She had crazy eyebrows, all bushy and black, just like Billy Batson, Captain Marvel's alter ego. When she laughed they waggled. That made Jack laugh. Pretty soon everyone was laughing, even the girl's brother, who had eyebrows almost as bushy and was about Jack's age. Many hands reached down to help Jack back up on his feet.

Still grinning, Jack picked up his bike and turned to make his way to the ferry. He stopped short. Right behind him stood his father, who had ridden the *Sam McBride* home from his job in the city.

"That was an amusing spectacle," said Mr. Gordon dryly.

"Well, sir, I didn't see the cart in time," said Jack, biting his lip.

"Indeed. Might you have seen it if you had been riding a little less recklessly, or perhaps looking where you were going?" Mr. Gordon cocked a black eyebrow, making him look quite stern. "Or maybe it would have been easier to avoid if you had been riding your other bike, the one that has all its parts."

"I like my trusty steed best," said Jack defiantly.

"So I see," replied his father. "Don't you have work to do?"

Jack had a summer job delivering the daily meat orders sent over from Pike's Butcher Shop on the mainland. With a last look at his father, Jack turned and began to load the packages into the basket wired to his back fender. So he didn't see the flicker of a smile on his father's face, a smile that looked suspiciously like Jack's grin in miniature.

Jack pedalled away with his load. He knew his father wasn't really angry, just *exasperated*. That was a new word for him. His mother used it all the time. When Jack asked her what it meant, she said it meant "Jack," which really didn't help him understand.

Jack turned down Withrow Street to start his route. There was a big field by the ferry docks. On one side of the field was the Clubhouse and on the other was the Wiman Shelter, which was a great place to meet friends. Past the field were the cottages. All the cottages on Ward's Island were at the far eastern end of the cluster of connected islands that made up the Toronto Islands. There were six north-south streets, and three east-west streets. Jack prided himself on being able to make all his deliveries in less than half an hour. Speed was important because the faster he made his deliveries, the faster the moms could start making supper. The faster that supper was over, the faster his crew could get out in their sailboats.

Jack checked the first package of meat. The hand-written label said that the Garnetts were having pork chops for dinner. He hopped on his trusty steed and headed towards their cottage on Willow Avenue. As he rode along, he thought about last night's camp-out. Captain Clapp was old, and had been working the lakers since he was Jack's age. He knew the wind and the waves better than anybody. When Jack's father got Jack his first boat, it was Captain Clapp who taught him to sail it. The Captain knew stuff. So his comments were still bothering Jack. He'd never do anything to hurt his friends. And most of the time he thought about what he was doing. It's just that he wasn't a wimp; he didn't mind getting into trouble and he always took his punishment like a man. That's what counted, wasn't it? Taking it like a man? His friends admired him. They followed him because Jack always had the best ideas.

He'd thought about it all night, and decided how he'd prove himself to the Captain. There was a big sailing regatta planned for the end of the summer. Sailboats came from Oakville and Montreal and even the United States to race in it. Jack was going to win the Cup. That would prove he was the best.

Jack grinned to himself as he knocked on the Garnett's door. He liked being the best.

CHAPTER 4
Jack and the New Kids

JACK WHISTLED AS HE FINISHED HIS DELIVERIES
and headed back to his cottage. The label on the
Gordons' package of meat said "ground beef." That
probably meant it was meat loaf for his dinner
tonight. As his mother worked in the kitchen, Jack
added a few boating pages to his cigar box and did a
bare minimum of cleaning up. He was just going to
get dirty again, wasn't he? His mother didn't understand that. When dinner came, Jack wolfed it down, in
spite of his mother's admonitions to use his manners.
This was the cottage, who needed manners? Then he
banged out the door, meaning to mount his trusty
steed and head to the Eastern Gap.

"Wait one minute, young man!" called his mother.
Groaning, Jack poked his head back around the screen

door. "A new family arrived today. They're renting the old Hanger place. I want you to take over a basket and introduce yourself. They've got a boy your age."

Jack's father chuckled. "I do believe Jack has already met the family," he said, looking askance at Jack. "Seems to me our son flew through the air and landed on their moving cart just this afternoon."

"Jack! You didn't! What will they think?"

Jack came back into the cottage to collect the basket, rolling his eyes at his father. "I didn't hurt anybody, Mom," he said. "Don't worry."

Taking the basket, Jack balanced it in his free hand as he pedalled over to the old Hanger place. The new family had just begun eating supper when he knocked at the door.

"Hi, I'm Jack Gordon," he said to the lady standing on the other side of the screen door. "I've got presents and stuff."

"I'm Mrs. Moffat. How very nice. Aren't you the boy who fell off his bike this afternoon? Are you all right?"

"No, ma'am, I didn't fall off my bike," replied Jack firmly. "I *meant* to do that. Like I said, I do it all the time and I never get hurt."

"I see." Smiling, Mrs. Moffat brought Jack into the kitchen. The girl with the funny eyebrows and the curly brown hair looked up curiously. She wasn't as young as Jack had originally thought. "Jack, this is my husband, Mr. Moffat, and my children, Charles and Lucy Mae."

"Hi. Yeah. Well, these are cookies. And things," said Jack, holding out the basket awkwardly. "They're from my mom and Missy Clapp. I'm to tell you 'welcome to Ward's Island.' My mom will probably come over to see you tomorrow, and take you to meet Missy Clapp. She doesn't visit; everybody visits her. She's pretty nice. She made the tollhouse cookies. Eat them, they're good, but don't eat the oatmeal cookies. My mom's not a very good baker."

Mrs. Moffat looked rather bemused at this speech, but took the basket from Jack anyway.

"Do you always eat this late?" Jack directed this question, rather bluntly, at Charles. "We're all done dinner. You'll miss everything if you don't hurry."

"What'll I miss?" asked Charles.

"We're going sailing, practicing for the big race. Have you got a boat? No? Well, you can watch from shore."

"You may be excused, Charles," said his father. "Don't be too late."

Charles took his plate to the sink, looking as if he wasn't entirely sure he wanted to go. Jack was moving a little fast for his taste. Was that how things worked on the island?

Jack slammed the screen door on the way out. Charles got his bike; his father had just bought him a brand new one. It was much nicer than Jack's battered contraption. Jack looked it over.

"Brand new, huh? Well, it won't take long to break it in. We've got a bicycle jump on Snake Island where you can speed down the ramp and fly into the lake. That should put a few scratches on it — give it a bit of character." Charles looked shocked. "Don't worry, the other boys and I'll get you some character right smartly." Charles frowned. He wasn't altogether sure he wanted any character.

Lucy Mae wolfed down the last few bites of her dinner and headed for the screen door. "Lucy Mae!" called her mother. "I'm sure some girls will be calling soon. The boys didn't say you could go with them."

"But they didn't say I couldn't!" retorted Lucy Mae, and she flew out the door.

CHAPTER 5
The Practice

"SO, ARE YOU STAYING ON THE ISLAND THE REST of the summer?" Jack called over his shoulder as the trio made their way to Clapp's Cove, just off the Eastern Gap.

"Yeah," replied Charles. "My dad has to work this summer so we can't take a real vacation. Our parents thought if we had a cottage it would almost seem like a holiday."

Charles sighed.

"Oh, summer on Ward's Island is pretty swell. There's all kinds of stuff to do. In the mornings we have Supervision. All the kids meet at the Shelter in the field by the water fountain and the Supervisor teaches stuff like swimming and diving and baseball and tennis."

Jack looked sideways at Lucy Mae. "The girls do

crafts like knitting and raffia weaving. Stuff like that." Jack was glad he wasn't a girl.

"And on the weekends the older boys play baseball and everybody watches the games. On Saturday night there's a dance and on Sunday a travelling minister comes to lead church services if your mom makes you go. Sometimes the singing's okay, I guess." Jack stopped for a quick breath.

"Ward's Island is attached to all the other Toronto Islands by bridges and there's different stuff to do on all of them. Sometimes we ride our bikes to Centre Island and have corn roasts on the beach and buy five-cent ice cream cones at the Dairy Bar. At Hanlan's Point we watch the planes take off from the Island Airport. And we go camping on Snake Island. We always have fun."

Charles was staring at Jack. All this boy seemed to do was talk.

"One thing, though," Jack went on. "We live pretty close together. So everybody knows everybody else's business. Which means when you get in trouble, you're in trouble with the whole island." Jack was clearly speaking from experience. He grinned. "There's one good thing about that. If you get hurt, there's a lot of mothers around to patch you back up!"

Jack hopped off his bike when they got to the Cove. Some boys were already pulling their boats down from the storage racks.

"We thought you weren't gonna make it, Jack," said one boy. "That'd be a first."

"This here is Charlie and — what's your name again?" Jack asked Lucy Mae. "Wait, I remember — Lucy, right? They're living in the old Hanger place. This here's my crew. Donnie, Dougie and Beans."

"Donnie's my right-hand man, my first mate. He can almost beat me sailing," Jack laughed. "But not quite!" Donnie was almost as tall as Jack, but had dark hair that flopped into his eyes. He wore funny suspenders and had holes in the knees of his dungarees.

"Missy Clapp named Beans — we can't remember what his real name is any more. It's cause of his hair; she thinks it looks like baked beans in the pot." Lucy Mae giggled. Beans was short and round and his head was covered with deep red curls. Someone had cut it so short that it did look like baked beans stuck all over his head.

"Dougie is Donnie's little brother. But stay away from him," laughed Jack, punching his friend in the shoulder. "He'll get you into trouble even faster than me!"

Charles looked overwhelmed. "It's Charles, actually," he said so quietly that no one heard. Lucy Mae stepped right into the knot of boys.

"Hi everybody!" she said brightly.

But nobody was listening. "Look, it's the *Cayuga*!"

A large, sleek vessel was steaming through the Eastern Gap. The *Cayuga* was one of the passenger steamships of the Great Lakes that treated passengers to a luxurious vacation while visiting ports of call in Canada and the United States. Smoke billowed from her two smokestacks. Her railings glittered with sparkling lights; her decks were awash with sound. As the *Cayuga* came closer, the island kids could make out the people in their evening clothes on the Promenade Deck; they could even see the dancers waltz to the big band sound of Harry Bedlington's Orchestra. The *Cayuga* passed like a dream, right before their eyes.

"They're drinking champagne," said Lucy Mae in wonder. "I can see their crystal glasses!"

"Just listen to that engine. Twin quadruple expansion, 328.75 horsepower!" Jack said in awe.

"It's like some other world," said Lucy Mae dreamily.

"It's MY world," retorted Jack. "I'm going to be captain of a ship like that, only bigger. And this here is my crew!" he went on, pointing to the other boys.

"Hey, you never know, Jack," shot back Donnie. "Maybe I'll be the captain and you'll be *my* crew!"

"Not blinking likely!" replied Jack. "You guys ready? I'll race you to the ferry dock and back! If you make the ferry captain move off his course, you get extra points!"

CHAPTER 6
Lucy Mae

JACK HAD LAUNCHED HIS BOAT AND WAS OFF before anyone else was ready.

"Did he really mean he was going to get in the way of the ferries?" asked Charles.

The crew laughed as they readied their own boats.

"Jackie thinks it's funny. Sailboats have right-of-way over boats with motors, even when the sailboat is as small as his and the motorboat is as big as a ferry. The ferry captains hate it."

"Well, I should think so," said Charles huffily. The other boys looked at one another. "Well," said Charles defensively, "it could be dangerous."

The other boys hooted with laughter. "Danger doesn't much bother Jackie," they guffawed. "And punishment is his middle name!" Then they were off, leaving Charles and Lucy Mae on the shore of the Cove.

Jack's boat was called *Frosty Friday*, because when he first asked for a sailboat his father had yelled, "It'll be a frosty Friday before you get a sailboat, young man!" But it wasn't too long before not one but two sailboats were delivered to the Gordon cottage.

"Maybe it'll keep you out of trouble," grumbled his father. "I had to get one too, just to keep an eye on you." Jack's mother sometimes wondered out loud which of her "boys" loved sailing the most.

The boats were ugly as sin. They looked like bathtubs with both ends cut off. Only eight feet long, they had steel daggerboards, rudders and single sails on a Marconi rigging. Some people thought the boats looked like wooden shoes, so they were called Sabot Prams, after the French word for wooden work shoes. Ugly or not, the prams were good work boats and could sail in any kind of weather.

Jack and the crew were soon lost to sight. Lucy Mae decided that watching sailboats from shore was pretty boring. Maybe she should have waited around to see if there were any fun girls on the island after all.

Charles peered into the gathering twilight. "The ferry just made a sharp turn. Do you think that boy actually got into its way on purpose?" he asked his sister.

"How should I know?" replied Lucy Mae. "It looks to me like he's got the guts to try it anyway. Even if it isn't too smart."

It wasn't long before the crew arrived back in the Cove. Charles and Lucy Mae helped them haul their boats onshore.

"Where's Jack?" asked Lucy Mae.

"He'll probably stay out until it's too dark to see. Don't worry about him," replied Donnie. "Listen, we've got Supervision in the morning. Meet us at nine at the Shelter. See ya!" And the crew was gone. Charles turned to go as well. "Aren't you coming home? Dad said not to be late."

"I'll be there in a minute," replied Lucy Mae.

It was almost pitch black by the time Jack turned *Frosty Friday* in towards shore. He'd tied a little flashlight onto his mast as a running light. As Jack hauled his boat out of the water, he was surprised to see Lucy Mae waiting in the darkness.

"Your boat's really ugly," she said conversationally.

Jack scowled at her. "What's your name again?"

"Lucy Mae," she replied patiently. "Will you take me sailing tomorrow?"

"No," said Jack shortly. "It's bad luck to have a woman on board a boat. Everybody knows that."

"You're kidding! You don't really believe that, do you?" asked Lucy Mae in disbelief. "How do you know I won't be good luck?"

"Because women just aren't. It's the law of the sea. All sailors have to abide by the laws of the sea. If you don't believe me, ask Captain Clapp. He lives at 2 Channel Avenue and he used to captain a laker. He knows all about it."

Lucy Mae rolled her eyes.

"Anyway," Jack went on, "I have to practice for the regatta. I'm going to win the Cup. I'm the best sailor in the Cove Fleet, you know."

"Do tell," said Lucy Mae archly. "I suppose you're the best at everything on Ward's Island."

Jack considered this carefully.

"Yes, I am," he replied.

"And modest, too."

Jack gave her a black look. "You can come and watch me race." He turned towards home. "Decide for yourself."

Lucy Mae watched him go, deep in thought. She didn't think she liked Jack. But it looked like he was the kid at the centre of all the island activities, the kid who made the fun happen. So he was the one she needed to make her friend. Her brother always played by the rules; he was boring. Lucy Mae liked adventure. Being friends with Jack looked like it might be a big one.

CHAPTER 7
The Ford Woody
Detroit, Michigan
Thursday

HENRY WAITED ANXIOUSLY AT THE WINDOW. Any minute now his dad would be home from work. And he'd be driving their brand new car. A 1949 Woody Station Wagon, with an all-steel frame and a Colony Blue paint job. It was called a Woody because of the varnished wood panels that covered the steel frame, and it was the most expensive car that Ford had ever made. It was going to cost the whopping sum of two thousand dollars. It would knock the socks off the stupid kids on his stupid street. None of their dads had a Woody.

Henry peered through the lace curtains of the Addison family's neat suburban home. Dad would drive up the street from the left. He'd get out and admire the sight of the new station wagon in front of their house for a moment. Finally – finally – he would come inside and say, "Anybody want a ride?" Henry just had to wait a few more minutes.

But the minutes passed. Henry fidgeted. When Dad finally came around the corner, he was driving their old car, the one he'd taken to work that morning. There was no Woody.

Henry dashed out into the front yard. "Dad?"

Dad put his arm around Henry's shoulders. "Sorry, little man, but there'll be no car for us today. I went to the Ford dealership and they're very sorry, but they can't make the cars fast enough. Everybody seems to want a new station wagon."

Henry wrenched away from his father. "But you promised!" he cried. "I told everybody on the street you were bringing it home!"

Mr. Addison sighed. "I'm sorry, Henry, I'm really sorry. But there's nothing I can do."

"What about our vacation? We're supposed to load up the new car and go on vacation! We're going to pack our suitcases and the picnic basket and at lunch we'll put down the tailgate to make a table and eat right there at the car. And we're going to drive all the way to Washington, DC and I'm going to see the statue of President Lincoln!"

Henry stopped for breath. More quietly, he said, "Dad, you promised. It's all planned. You *have* to get our new station wagon."

"Sometimes things just don't work out as we plan, Son. The dealership didn't realize how many orders were being placed all over the country. It's good news really; all those car orders mean lots of jobs at the Ford plant where I work. And all those orders mean that we picked the right car, the best car, the one that everybody wants! We're pretty smart, aren't we?" Henry's dad tried to be jovial.

We already knew it was the best car, thought Henry. What good is that, if we can't have one?

"What about our vacation?" asked Henry sullenly. "Our old car will never make it to Washington. I'll have to sit around with nothing to do!"

"I've got a plan," said his father. "Come inside and I'll tell you and Mother all about it."

Mr. and Mrs. Addison talked quietly while Henry's mother made coffee. Henry sat at the kitchen table, waiting. He took the advertisement for the new car out of his pocket, where he always carried it. Carefully he flattened it out on the table.

It's a Dream Wagon...this '49 ford
with its heart of steel
and the new ford 'feel'!

Henry's heart felt like steel, cold and hard. Henry's parents brought their coffee over to the table, along with a bottle of soda for Henry.

GROVENOR LIBRARY

"I knew you'd be disappointed, Henry, so when I heard about the car I made a few phone calls. I've got us booked on an even more exciting vacation – we're going to go on a boat trip! There are all kinds of cruises on the Great Lakes, right at our doorstep. We'll have our own room on the boat – it's called a state-room – and we'll eat our meals in a beautiful dining room with fine china and waiters serving us, and there will be bands and dancing and card games and lots of things to do. And the scenery will be beautiful. Doesn't that sound like fun?"

Dancing. Card games. Scenery. Oh sure, that really sounded like a fun summer vacation. Way more fun than tailgate picnics, the Lincoln Memorial and the FORD 'FEEL.' Didn't his dad understand? No boat could compare with a brand new car. Angrily, Henry crumpled the car advertisement and threw it on the floor.

His father rubbed his temples, and sighed. "I booked the biggest and best steamboat I could find. Her name's the *Noronic*, and she's known as the 'Queen of the Inland Seas.' She crosses Lake Erie, puts in at Cleveland then goes through the locks at the Welland Canal right into Lake Ontario. She stops in Toronto then steams past a castle in the Thousand Islands. It'll be great, Henry."

Henry didn't answer. He was sulking.

Henry's father opened his briefcase and pulled out an advertisement. He slid it across the kitchen table to Henry.

On the "Noronic" for a Week —
Together Far-Off Ports We Seek
Come Sail with Us for a Wonderful Week
Over the Glorious Inland Seas

"It'll be fun, Henry," repeated his father anxiously. "You'll see."

"Why should I believe you?" retorted Henry.

"Henry, a lot of children don't get to go on holidays at all," said his mother quietly. "You should feel lucky."

"Well, I don't!" With that, Henry shoved the advertisement onto the floor. "This will be a stupid, boring holiday!"

Sadly, Henry's father took the *Noronic* advertisement, folded it carefully and put it in a drawer.

CHAPTER 8
Henry Has an Adventure
Friday

HENRY WAS BORED. THERE WAS NOTHING TO do. It was the worst summer vacation ever. He dragged into the kitchen and draped himself over a chrome kitchen chair. Henry's mother didn't appear to notice him. He sighed dramatically. His mother still didn't react.

"I'm bored," Henry sulked.

"So I guessed," replied his mother in a matter-of-fact voice.

"What can I do?"

"It's summer vacation, Henry," his mother replied patiently. "You can do pretty much what you'd like."

"There's nothing *to* do," whined Henry.

"Why don't you visit your friends?"

"Don't have any," said Henry grumpily.

"You could ride your bike to the library and get some books to read," suggested his mother.

"Don't want to. Will you take me to the movies?"

"No, I won't. But if you've truly nothing to do, you could help me. Why don't you push the vacuum over the broadloom then dust the figurines in the china cabinet?"

Henry glared at his mother. She raised her eyebrow at him. "If you don't want to work, then go play. Kindly do it without whining."

Henry scowled and went out onto the back porch. He was small for his age with pale, nearly white skin. Next to his dark hair and eyes, this paleness made Henry look a little sickly. He had in fact had a rough beginning in life, spending most of his first three years in hospital while doctors worked on his heart. It was just fine now, but his parents tended to baby him. This hadn't helped Henry make friends; all the other kids thought he was a spoiled brat. Which was pretty close to the truth.

The toys Henry's parents regularly bought cluttered the backyard. His bicycle leaned against the garden shed. The swing set swayed in the slight breeze. A baseball bat was tangled in the lilac bush and a football lay half buried in the sandbox. He was so bored.

Henry sighed loudly a few more times, just in case his mother decided to take him to the movies after all. But the only sound coming from the kitchen was the

Mixmaster. Slowly, Henry kicked his way down the back steps to the lawn and wheeled his bike to the driveway. Throwing one leg over the seat, Henry began to pedal a tad unsteadily down Ravine Street. He wasn't sure of his destination, but who cared?

Right, then left and left again. Henry's pedalling became stronger. He pedalled farther than he was allowed to go. He pedalled along the neat suburban streets until the houses were replaced with small shops. There were more cars on the road, so Henry watched for Ford Dream Wagons. The shops turned into factories. All of a sudden Henry stopped. He wasn't exactly sure where he was. It would serve his mother right if he was lost.

Up ahead, Henry could see water. He was at the Port of Detroit. His mother would be furious. Good, thought Henry nastily.

Pushing his bike closer to the water, Henry looked around. The port was actually pretty swell. Huge cranes lifted cargo onto freighters. Diggers worked in dusty piles of black coal. Ropes as thick as Henry's leg lay coiled all about. Tiny men scurried along rickety gangplanks into the holds of the big freighters, looking like ants.

And the boats! They were colossal. Some towered five stories above him. Surely they were too big to float? Huge smokestacks belched black smoke into the air. The movement of the water rocked the massive beasts, making their ropes tighten, their chains clank and their hulls squeal as they rubbed against the dock pilings. There was so much noise and smoke. It felt dangerous, and exciting. Henry shivered. These were the great lake boats, destined for ports all over the world.

And he was going to ride on one.

Thoughts of the Ford Dream Wagon faded into the back of his mind. He strained to recall the picture of the *Noronic* from the brochure. One smokestack or two? Black or white hull? Was she here? Henry hopped back on his bike, recovered from a wobble, and set off in search of *his* boat.

From out of nowhere, an enormous hand reached down from the sky and grabbed Henry's suspenders, lifting him into the air. His bike crashed to the ground. Legs dangling in mid-air, Henry's hands flailed about searching for something – anything – to grab on to. There was nothing. He stopped wiggling and slowly looked up. A huge black man held Henry aloft, just as if he were a stray kitten. The man's shirt was streaked with coal dust and sweat, and barely covered the muscles in his arms and chest; muscles even bigger than Popeye's. And the man looked mad.

CHAPTER 9
The Curse

"JUST WHERE DO YA THINK YOU'RE GOIN'?" growled the man.

Henry's tongue was frozen. He was terrified.

"Little punks, gettin' in the way," mumbled the man under his breath. He lowered Henry to the ground. Terror made Henry's legs give out on him, and he sank into a heap next to the giant's workboots.

"Oh, for heck's sake!" exploded the man, grabbing Henry's suspenders once more and hauling him to his feet. "Stand up, will ya, I don't bite!" Henry stood up.

"Now, you look like a nice little boy, and nice little boys have no business down here. The docks is too busy a place for us dock workers to be lookin' out for the likes of you. Go home now, home to your mama."

Henry wanted nothing more. But he *did* have business down at the docks and felt the need to make that clear to the irate man.

"I'm looking for my boat. I'm going to be sailing on one of these ships and I wanted to see what she looked like," stated Henry with just a little quiver in his voice. "That's my business here at the docks."

"Sir," he added, hoping that would help his case.

The big man squatted down to Henry's level. His skin was so black it was almost blue and he looked very fierce as he stared at Henry. Then his mouth opened and he laughed, right out loud, showing a magnificent set of white teeth.

"First of all, there's lots of folks around here will tell you I ain't no 'sir,' so you can't call me that. I'm Moses. Second, these here are called boats, not ships. If they travelled the saltwater oceans they'd be ships, but they work the freshwater of the Great Lakes so they're boats. Third, these boats got no sails, they're steamboats, so you won't be doing no sailing. And fourth, the boats here at this dock are freighters. They don't take no passengers. You got a lot of stuff wrong in just one sentence, boy. Even Moses knows more than you, and I ain't never been to school."

Moses was still chuckling as he stood up. He picked up Henry's bike and handed it back to him.

"So what boat you travellin' on?"

"The *Noronic*," replied Henry.

"The *Norey*? She's a good ol' girl," said Moses.

"You've seen her?" asked Henry anxiously.

"Course I seen her," said Moses proudly. "I work all the docks. The *Norey*'s famous in these parts."

"Why is she famous?" asked Henry.

"Well, folks like her cause she's the biggest of the passenger boats. Pretty fancy inside and the whiskey flows real good. Ya know what I mean, kid?"

Henry didn't, but he nodded.

"But that's the stuff the rich folks know. Us down here at the docks, we know more'n that."

"Like what?" prompted Henry.

"They built her wrong. They added a deck when they shouldn't have and it made her tippy. She went right over the first time they tried to load her."

"My mom won't like it if she's tippy," said Henry dubiously.

"Not to worry. They fixed her just fine. Made her wider. Put pig iron in the hold to keep her steady. Your mama will be fine."

"What else do you know?" insisted Henry.

"The *Norey* carries a boatload of luck."

"That's good, isn't it?" persisted Henry.

Moses squatted down again and looked at Henry eyeball to eyeball. "There's two kinds of luck, little man. Good luck and bad luck. The *Norey* has a hold full of both. And ya never know which you're going to get."

Henry was thoughtful a moment. "Tell me about the good luck."

"That's easy," said Moses. "She should have gone down her first day. It was November, 1913. I remember it, even though I was just a little kid like you. The *Norey* was half finished, and she was meant to steam down to Sarnia for the winter so the carpenters could finish all the inside cabins and whatnot. But the winds blew up the day before she was to leave. 'Go anyway,' the shipbuilders said. 'It's just the Gales of November. We get storms like that every year.' But the owner says, 'No. Wait.' Turns out that storm was the worst ever. For four days it was like a hurricane. Nowadays when they talk about that time, they call it the White Hurricane." Moses paused for effect.

"The storm coulda took the *Norey* that week. But it didn't. That's the good luck."

"What about the bad luck, Moses?" asked Henry.

"Well…" Moses hesitated.

"Tell me!"

Moses looked around to see if anyone was listening. "Once there was some stowaways on board, and they got caught. When they were put off, they were real mad. Kid, them stowaways put a curse on your boat."

CHAPTER 10
Henry Gets Interested

MENTION OF THE CURSE MADE MOSES'S expression get all fierce again. It was almost as if he wished he hadn't said anything.

"Ain't you got a library card? You want more, you find out for yourself, kid," grunted Moses. "Now, git outta here before you get hurt!"

Henry git.

Retracing his route as best he could, Henry found his way home. But he didn't stop there; he pedalled straight on past to the public library. He must have pulled a hundred books off the shelves, but hard as he looked, nowhere could Henry find any mention of the curse. He did find lots of other stuff about the *Noronic*, though, and carefully copied it all down on some paper the librarian gave him. Once home, he

looked in all the drawers until he found his dad's
Noronic brochure. He took it, then put all the papers
away in the strongbox he'd insisted his mother buy for
him. It kept his important stuff. His secret stuff.

At dinner, Henry didn't complain once about his
dinner. He even ate his canned peas.

"Mom," asked Henry between bites, "have you
ever thought about taking all the labels off the cans so
that we wouldn't know what's for dinner?"

Both Henry's mother and father looked at him
with surprise. "Why on earth would we do that?"
asked his mother.

"Wouldn't it be fun?" Henry went on. "I was
doing some reading about the *Noronic* today. You
know, at the library?" Henry was sure his parents
would be unhappy to hear about his visit to the docks.

"You were reading about the *Noronic*? At the
library?" Mr. and Mrs. Addison looked at one another
in surprise.

"Her cargo hoist doesn't work very well. Once she
was being loaded and the hoist failed and dumped all
the cans of food that were supposed to be for the passengers into the lake. A whole bunch of kids went
down to the docks and waited until she steamed away,
then they dove into the lake and rescued the tins. But
the labels had soaked off. So they didn't know what
was for dinner! I think that would be swell. We could
call it 'supper surprise.'"

"I don't think it would be 'swell' at all," retorted his mother. "Don't get any funny ideas."

"Why this sudden interest in the *Noronic*, Henry?" asked his dad suspiciously. "Last I heard you were too angry about the car to care one fig about our boat trip."

"Well, I heard some stuff that made me change my mind. I'm allowed to change my mind, aren't I?! Did you know that she was designed by a Swedish man? And that he designed the *Kingston* and the *Cayuga* too? And that the *Kingston* and the *Cayuga* are both going to be in port in Toronto on the same night we are? That's what they call a co-rinky-dink."

"Do you mean *coincidence*?" asked his dad, looking a little confused.

"What I said. The *Noronic's* 362 feet long, and she's got five decks. And you know how she got her name? It's because when they started building her she was owned by the Northern Navigation Company up in Canada. They always named their boats something that ended in 'ic.' But by the time they finished building her, that company had merged with another company called the Richelieu and Ontario Line. So they called her the NO – R – ON – IC after the merger. I'll bet you didn't know that, Dad." Henry stopped for breath.

"You're right, Henry. I didn't know that." Mr. Addison looked at Mrs. Addison with bemusement. This was a new Henry. They didn't know where he'd come from, but he was sure easier to get along with than the old one.

"And Mom, you know how you like to do spring cleaning?" Mrs. Addison nodded, wondering what that had to do with steamboats.

"Well, you should try doing it on the *Noronic*! It's a really big job. They start by scrubbing her from top to bottom with 'soogey.' You know what that is? It's this horrible mix of soap, soda, soogey powder and Gilette's Lye. It gets boiled until it's red-hot, then the men have to scrub the ship with it. I'll bet their hands darn near get burnt right off from that boiling lye. Then they have to paint. They use gallons and gallons of paint and turpentine. And oil – they have to add lots of oil to the hull paint to preserve it."

"Gallons and gallons of paint and oil?" laughed Mr. Addison. "It sounds more like a paint factory than a ship, Henry."

"It makes it shine, Dad," Henry said defensively. The *Noronic's* the Queen, and she always has to shine. I heard…I mean, I read…that she's a good luck ship. I'm glad you picked her, Dad. This'll be a fun vacation."

Henry excused himself from the table. His parents couldn't believe the change in his attitude. They wondered what had made him so excited.

There was no way they could guess that it was a curse.

CHAPTER 11
Race Day
Toronto Islands
Saturday

S ATURDAY WAS RACE DAY. IT WAS JUST A RACE for the Ward's Island sailors, but it was good practice for the big regatta. The islanders called themselves the Cove Fleet because they sailed out of Clapp's Cove. Captain Clapp was Commodore of the Fleet, Jack's dad was Race Chairman and Beans's dad headed up the Protest Committee. It was all organized by international rules; the islanders took their sailing very seriously.

The moms were setting out sandwiches and lemonade for all the folks who were coming to watch the regatta. Everybody came to the races. Each sailor wiped his boat down then fiddled with it, trying to squeeze out the tiny bit of extra speed that could win or lose a race. The competitive spirit reared up in each captain; each secretly studied what the others were doing.

"So how does the race work?" asked Lucy Mae. Jack looked up with surprise. He'd been so busy working on *Frosty Friday* that he hadn't noticed her.

"Well, the judges lay out three markers about a quarter mile apart in sort of a triangle. Each marker is made of a giant, empty soup tin — we got one tomato and three vegetable — and four sticks of wood, all about five feet long. The sticks are tied at the top and the bottom, then the soup can is stuck in the middle, so the wood bulges in the middle and makes it float. The top of the markers have got a flag, so we can see them from a ways off and the bottoms are tied to an anchor. My dad made them.

"All we got to do is sail around the markers. But to do it, we got to tack. That means we don't sail directly there. The wind usually won't let us go direct to the marker, so we have to angle towards it, sailing on one side then the other. When you tack, you want to sail as close to the wind as you can, because then your angles aren't too wide and you get there faster. Got it?"

"Not really," said Lucy Mae dubiously.

"I'll draw it out," replied Jack. He was truly serious about his sailing. Jack dug two holes in the sand with his toe.

"Here's your boat," he said pointing to one. "And here's the marker. You can't get there in a straight line because the wind is usually blowing in a different direction. So you have to zigzag." Jack dragged his foot back and forth across the line. "The smaller your zigzags, the faster you'll get there. So you want to sail as close to the line as you can. That's called close-hauling. But if you sail too close, you'll lose your wind. So you got to be careful."

Lucy Mae nodded. That made sense.

"Then you got to get around the markers. That's where a race will be won or lost. There's all kinds of rules about it. It's too complicated to explain. I gotta go."

Jack made a last adjustment to his sail and pushed *Frosty Friday* off the beach. Soon there were twenty or so prams bobbing on the water, white sails taut in the breeze. And one red sail. It belonged to *Frosty Friday*.

Jack's white pea cap gleamed in the sun. He was in his element, bright blue eyes peering at the cat's paws in the water. Cat's paws were small patches of dark in the water, caused by light winds ruffling the surface and changing the reflection of the sun. Nobody, except maybe the Captain, could read them as well as Jack could, to determine the direction and strength of the wind.

He tacked to port then starboard, testing the wind as the judges' boat putted out from shore. The judges' boat was called the *Shepherd*. It was just a little rowboat with a tiny motor that all the Ward's Islanders had chipped in to buy. Ross Leitch, who operated the island water taxi, John Van Camp, who owned the pushcart, and Honey Jackson, Donnie and Dougie's dad, were in it. Their job was to set the course and rule on any protests after the race. And rescue anybody who dumped, of course.

The sailors jockeyed for position at the start line. Jack was aiming for a buck start; he wanted to tack upwind. It took skill to be correctly positioned at the line, without going over. The ten-minute flag was hoisted on the *Shepherd*. Jack set his stopwatch. Time for a nervous pee. Jack pulled his centreboard out and peed into the lake down the centreboard box. He slammed his board back into place, just as Dougie did the same in the next boat. They grinned at one another. The five-minute flag went up. Donnie was edging him over the line. One minute. Jack fought to stay behind the line. The starting pistol went off.

Jack and *Frosty Friday* were like a single creature when they raced. Jack hardly even used the rudder; he could steer the boat just by shifting his weight. *Frosty Friday* did just what she was told. Jack didn't even bother using a tickler to read the wind. Ticklers were tiny ribbons some captains attached to their bows.

They annoyed Jack; he could read the wind just by watching the direction of the cat's paws in the water. If they got dark, a gust was coming. He knew about it before it even arrived, so he was always ready to take advantage. Every puff belonged to him and *Frosty Friday*.

The prams tacked in tight formation on the first leg of the race. There was no room to manoeuvre, so they came onto the first marker in a pack. Jack watched the other sailors. The chickens would go wide to stay out of trouble. They'd end up nice and safe at the back of the pack. The competitors would push close to the mark. Closest one would have overlap and the right-of-way, forcing the others to hang back. Jack was determined to be that boat. The danger lay in cutting it too close, and missing the marker altogether. Then he'd have to turnabout and try again. The race would be lost.

Beans, Jack and Donnie were flying towards the marker as a threesome. Donnie was closest to the mark. Jack allowed himself to be blanketed by Beans's boat. *Frosty Friday* lost wind and fell back, just a bit. Just enough for Jack to get in behind Donnie's boat then slip round the other side, squeezing himself between Donnie and the marker.

"Buoy room, buoy room!" yelled Jack. "I've got overlap!"

Donnie had no choice but to fall back and let Jack in.

Once round the marker, Jack was well in the lead. Behind him Beans and Donnie were still trying to recover from Jack's strategy. Jack found a fairing on the second leg, a good channel that allowed him to tack close to the wind. He rounded the second and third marks alone and flew home, first over the finish line.

Just like always.

CHAPTER 12
The Winner

THERE WERE THREE RACES THAT AFTERNOON. Jack won all of them. As the prams were put away, Jack teased the other captains.

"Donnie, you could have had me in that first race! I know I'm the skinniest, but boy, you sure let me slide through on that overlap."

"Hey Dougie, what, you got pig iron in your boat? You were slow as molasses out there today!"

The other boys were quiet. Jack was a lot of fun most of the time, but man, he sure got competitive. It turned him into a different person. The boys drifted off towards home and supper until only Lucy Mae was left.

"So, am I the best?" asked Jack smugly.

"At what?" retorted Lucy Mae. "If you mean sailing, then yes, you're the best. But you don't need me to tell you that. You're too busy telling everybody yourself."

"Hey, they're my buddies. We're just having fun. They don't like losing, that's all."

Lucy Mae wasn't so sure. But Jack really had been something to watch out there. Sailing was hard to watch from shore, but even at that distance she could see how the red sail flew across the water. The other boats had looked like sitting ducks; *Frosty Friday* had been more like a water spider, darting in and out and around the fat birds.

Jack finished up with *Frosty Friday*. "I gotta get my meat deliveries done. Tell Charlie I'll pick him up tomorrow. We're going to Centre Island for ice cream."

"Can I come?" asked Lucy Mae directly.

"Anybody can go get ice cream," Jack looked surprised. "You can do whatever you want."

"How do you do it?" asked Lucy Mae. "Sail like that?"

Jack started into a spiel. "Because I'm the best!" Then he looked, for the first time, directly at Lucy Mae. She really wanted to know.

"It's like chess," Jack said slowly. "You're one of the pieces. You have to be in control of your piece, you have to know how to make it move where you want it to go. Once you know that, you have to look at the other pieces. Where are they on the board? How are they going to move? Who's going to knock you off the board?" Jack stopped. "You win if you can guess where all the pieces are going to be."

Lucy Mae was impressed. "How did you learn that?"

"Part of it I learned from Captain Clapp. He knows wind, and boats and currents. Part of it I just know; I don't know how. When I'm on the water, I just know I'm meant to be there."

Jack straddled his trusty steed. "Tomorrow if you come for ice cream, we'll go see Captain and Missy Clapp after. You'll like them." Jack started pedalling away. "And don't forget to tell Charlie."

Lucy Mae ran after him. "He doesn't like to be called Charlie!"

Jack grinned over his shoulder. "Too bad. He's an islander now!"

CHAPTER 13
Getting Character
Sunday

B Y THE TIME THE BOYS AND LUCY MAE MET at the Shelter the next day, the races had been forgotten. With Jack and his trusty steed leading the way, they pedalled for all they were worth in the direction of Centre Island. They passed the bridge to Algonquin Island and were nearing Snake Island when Jack abruptly changed course.

"We gotta go to the jump first!" yelled Jack. "C'mon!" All the bikes thundered over the bridge to Snake Island, then stopped.

"Where's Charlie?" asked Jack. "C'mon up."

Slowly Charles walked his bike towards Jack. "What?" he asked cautiously.

"I promised to give your bike some character. This here's the jump. You just ride as fast as you can down the path till you get to that little dock up ahead. See the ramp there? We built it just for this. Ride up the ramp. It's best to be standing up for that part. When you go off the end of the ramp, make sure you let go so the bike falls first. You'll fly right over it. It's great. You'll see."

Charles was dumbfounded. "You're kidding, right?"

"It's really fun," Jack assured him. "We'll go first, so you can see how it's done."

One by one, Donnie, Dougie, Beans and Jack flew off the ramp amid great whoops and splashes. It really did look like fun. But still Charles hesitated. Lucy Mae looked at her brother. Then at the ramp. With a determined look on her face, she got on her bike and pedalled hard. In moments she was flying through the air, absolutely terrified. Her bike dropped from beneath her; seconds later she hit the water with a crash. She came up spluttering.

"That was great!" she exclaimed.

Charles had no choice any more. With resignation, he got on his brand new bike and aimed for the dock. Faster and faster he went, then up and in.

Shaking the water from his hair, he pulled his bike out of the lagoon. The front fender had a dent and there were scratches all over the frame. And Charles was grinning from ear to ear.

"There, man. Now you got character! Onward,

lads!" The crew hopped back onto their bikes and continued to Centre Island and the Dairy Bar.

Lucy Mae was still sipping her milkshake when the boys finished slurping theirs down.

"Back to Ward's, crew. Let's visit the Captain," called Jack, and once again they were off. By the time they made it back to the Shelter, there was a baseball practice in full swing. They stayed to watch for a few minutes, debating the merits of the island teams. There were four: the Otazels, the Osoezes, the Brownies and the Dingbats. The consensus was that the Osoezes would win the Island Championship that summer. Having decided that, they were back on their bikes and making their way to 2 Channel Avenue. The Captain and Missy Clapp were sitting on their front porch.

"Look what the storm dragged in, Missy," growled the Captain. "A whole lot of wet dogs. And one cat, it appears. You must be the new girl at the Hanger place, right?"

Lucy Mae nodded. "Yes sir," she replied politely. "I'm Lucy Mae Moffat and that's my brother Charles."

"That so?" said the Captain. "Now, little missy, I'm not 'sir,' I'm the Captain. Always was, always will be. Born to the inland sea. Like our Jack here. We got water in our veins instead of blood. What do you all need the Captain for tonight?"

"Captain, tell us about the ghost. Charles and Lucy Mae *need to be warned*," said Jack dramatically.

"Don't mess around, young Jack Gordon. That ghost ain't going to eat nobody," admonished the Captain. "But he may well scare you to death," he added gravely. "Are you sure you want to hear it?"

The kids all settled down on the porch steps, eyes wide. Missy Clapp sent Beans into the cottage to fetch the lantern, her knitting and her ever-full cookie tin. She settled back into her porch rocker with a smile.

CHAPTER 14
A Good Captain

"It was January, 1815. Mr. J.P. Rademuller was the lightkeeper at the Gibraltar Point lighthouse. You kids know the one, down past Centre near the dogleg turn that heads towards Hanlan's Point. He was a German fellow. I'm told he made a right fine beer and was known through the lakes for his skill. Well, that night in January, Mr. Rademuller up and disappeared. He was never seen again. Folks came over to look when the light didn't go on, but no Rademuller."

"They sent another lightkeeper. And another. Every one of them heard strange sounds in the lighthouse. Like heels being dragged up the steps. Bump. Drag. Bump. Drag. But nothing was ever seen. Not for seventeen years. Then one day the keeper was digging in his garden, when the shovel hit something hard. He dug it up. You boys know what it was, don't you?"

"A skull," Dougie breathed. "A *human* skull."

"That's right. And the rest of the bones followed. The keeper knew who it was all right. Rademuller. Seems like some soldiers from over at Fort York got drunk one night. Went to the lighthouse for more beer. Rademuller said they'd had enough and offered to let them sleep it off at the lighthouse. Those soldiers weren't ready for sleeping. Not one bit. They smashed Rademuller over the head with a piece of his own firewood, dragged his body up the steps to the top of the lighthouse and threw him over. But he didn't wash away, now, did he? They had to bury him.

"They never caught the soldiers. So Rademuller can't rest easy. You can still hear his heels bump each step as he's dragged up those steps." The Captain looked around. All the kids were wide-eyed, except for one.

"Is that really true?" asked Charles skeptically.

The Captain eyeballed Charles. "Only way to find out is to stay the night in the lighthouse, and none of you would be fool enough to do that, now would you?"

"Don't you give these young people any ideas, Captain," scolded Missy Clapp. The Captain regarded his audience with a twinkle in his eyes. "I wouldn't do that, now would I?" He laughed.

"Were you ever in a really bad storm, Captain?" asked Lucy Mae. "One that scared you?"

The Captain laughed. "I've been in more than one that scared me, I'll tell you that. But the worst was in 1913. The November gales came in hard and heavy that year. For four days it was like a hurricane, one with snow and ice on top of wind, but the Weather Service refused to call it that because they said hurricanes only happen in the tropics. Huh! Shows what they know. Winds were blowing ninety miles an hour, waves were thirty-five feet high, snow was blowing so hard you couldn't see ten feet in front of you. Men froze to the rigging that year.

"I was working the passenger ship *Illinois*. We were lucky; our captain drove the bow of our ship onto the shore of South Manitou Island, tied us to a tree and we rode it out. Others weren't so lucky. The storm gave 250 men to the Great Lakes that week. Twenty-eight boats, big, like the freighters here, were wrecked. And eleven more went straight to the bottom, where they still lie.

"And the White Hurricane — that's what they call the Gale of 1913 now — gave us a fine mystery, boys. Figure this one out: two of the boats that went down with all hands were the freighter *Regina* and the ore carrier *Charles S. Price*. The *Regina* was never found. The *Price* was. But the bodies of the *Price* crew were wearing lifejackets from the *Regina*. And nobody knows how that happened."

There were whistles from the boys. "You never told us that before, Captain!"

Lucy Mae's eyes were large. "Why did you work the Great Lakes if it's so dangerous?" she asked.

The Captain laughed. "The lakes get in your blood, young missy. You just got to respect them. This is an inland sea. It's so big it has tides, just like the ocean. And storms just like the ocean. Waves can go over the bow, snow squalls can make a sailor blind, ice can crush a freighter into matchsticks. Make no mistake, the Great Lakes can be wicked."

"But the big lakers can take it, can't they, Captain?" Jack piped in.

"The lakers are grand vessels, Jack, but don't get cocky. Each and every one is at the mercy of the lakes. Even the best captains are afraid of storms."

"But they're not afraid of anything else, are they, Captain?" insisted Jack. "A laker captain is like a king!"

"Sometimes when you stand at the helm it feels like that, young Jack. But like I said, don't get cocky. A good captain is afraid of two things. One of them is a bad storm, a November gale. The other is fire. A fire on board is a captain's worst nightmare. And don't you forget it."

CHAPTER 15
Jack Picks a Queen

"I SAID YOU'D LIKE THE CAPTAIN AND MISSY Clapp," said Jack, as the kids made their way to the Shelter. "The Captain knows everything about the Great Lakes. And Missy Clapp makes the best cookies, don't you think?"

Lucy Mae was thoughtful. "Jack, how can you want to be a captain if it's so dangerous?"

"It's only dangerous sometimes. And the rest of the time you feel like a king, even the Captain said so," replied Jack. "And besides, it's like I said earlier." Jack dropped back and lowered his voice so he was talking just to Lucy Mae. "When I'm on the water, I can see where the pieces are supposed to be. When I'm on land, it's not so easy."

Jack ran ahead to catch up to the others. "Why don't we get the ukes?"

There was a smattering of "Yeah, let's" and "Good idea" thrown into the wind as the boys dashed in all directions to collect their ukuleles. Lucy Mae ran home to tell her mother where they were.

"Thanks, dear," Mrs. Moffat replied. "But I'm not worried. I was talking to Mrs. Gordon — you know, Jack's mother — today, and she told me that the island kids look after each other pretty well, so they're usually allowed to stay out after dark. Just don't you and Charles leave the group, all right?"

Was this her mother speaking? In the city she never let them stay out after dark. Lucy Mae dashed back to the Shelter before her mother could change her mind.

By the time she arrived, most of the boys had returned and were tuning up their ukuleles. Finally everyone settled down and began to strum.

First it was "Bye Bye Blackbird," then "Junior Birdsman." By the time the boys got to "Leaning on a Lamppost" everybody was singing. When they got tired, they put one of George Formby's records on the phonograph and tried to pick out his chords. Formby was a big star and made a boatload of money playing his ukulele. Jack showed his instrument to Charles and Lucy Mae.

"I got Formby to autograph my uke when he played in Toronto at the Royal Alexandra Theatre," he said proudly. "Look."

It was getting late. "Last song," called Dougie. "Let's do 'The Titanic.'" Even Charles and Lucy Mae knew the words to that one, so when it came time for the chorus the whole group belted it out.

Oh, it was sad,
Mighty sad,
It was sad when the great ship went down
To the bottom. All the husbands and wives
Little children lost their lives.
It was sad
When the great ship went down.

They were all still laughing as they left the Shelter to make their way home. "Look, Jack!" shouted Beans, pointing towards the city. "The pier's full!" They all looked. It was true. The pier at the foot of Yonge Steet, just across the harbour, was ablaze with lights.

"Which ones? Can you tell?" asked Donnie.

Jack peered through the dark. "Looks like the *Cayuga*, the *Dalhousie*, the *Northumberland*…and maybe even the *Kingston*!"

"That's a full house for sure," said Dougie. "Never seen it like that before, have you, Jack?"

Jack shook his head, his gaze fixed on the big lakers.

"Which one's your favourite?" asked Lucy Mae.

"The *Noronic*. She's not there. She's the biggest, and

the best," replied Jack, "but she only comes to Toronto once a year. Late in the season."

"What does she look like?" pressed Lucy Mae.

"Well, I've never actually seen her, but I reckon she's worth waiting for. Captain says she's got a strange whistle, so you can tell she's coming from miles away. She's got one smokestack and a crow's nest. She's the only passenger boat that's got one. Captain says you can't miss her. This year I'm listening for her. This year I'll see her for sure. You see, she's going to be my ship one day. And when I get her, maybe then I'll let you sail with me."

CHAPTER 16
Bicycle Polo
Monday

"Bye, Mom!" Jack banged the screen door on his way out the next morning. "Beans? Come on!!!"

The screen door of the next house over banged shut. "I'm coming!" yelled Beans. The two boys hopped on their bikes and headed off at a dead tear.

"If we're fast, we can get in a quick game of bicycle polo before Supervision," called Jack. "Let's go to the Shelter."

"Right," replied Beans as he followed in Jack's energetic wake, pedalling vigorously. Jack swerved onto Fifth Street. "We'd better pick up the new kid," he yelled over his shoulder.

Charles wasn't ready. Jack bullied him into wolfing

down his cereal and hurried him out the door. "Boy, you're slow!" Jack exclaimed.

The rest of the crew was already batting a rubber ball back and forth. All of them had brought sticks of some sort. Beans had a baseball bat; Donnie and Dougie had "borrowed" mallets from their Dad's croquet set and Jack had a hockey stick, although it was broken in two places and held together with black electrical tape. They lent Charles an old lacrosse stick and left him to figure out the rules on his own.

Diving into the game, Jack soon had control of the ball, walloping it in Dougie's direction. Dougie whacked it into goal. A cheer went up. Beans skidded past in a tight turn, dragging his baseball bat along the grass then swinging for a long shot. A miss. Donnie made a smooth recovery, riding fast and hard, leaning far to the left for a wide shot to goal. The shot was good, but Donnie's bike slid out from under him, dumping him on his head with an audible crack. Donnie untangled himself from his bike, staring glumly at the broken fender.

"My bike's got a war wound!" he shouted. "Two points for my team!"

Just then the low whistle of the *Sam McBride* sounded. The play heated up; only a few more minutes before the morning supervisor arrived. Charles got a lucky goal with his lacrosse stick, which promptly broke in half. Jack passed to Beans, who passed to

Dougie, who lost the ball to Donnie, who passed it to Jack. The *Sam McBride* was in; there was no time left. Jack swung hard with his stick for one last shot on goal. Too hard. The rubber ball went sailing into the air, right into the middle of the crowd coming off the ferry.

Jack groaned. Sheepishly, he dropped his bike and walked over to the crowd to collect the ball.

"You're not a very good shot, are you?" came Lucy Mae's voice from behind him.

"Course I am, when I want to be," retorted Jack. "People remember me better when I do something funny."

"Even when it's stupid? Even when you could have hit someone?"

"I already have enough mothers; I don't need you," Jack threw back, and returned to the Shelter. The crew appeared by magic, ribbing him about his last shot. Over their heads, Jack grinned at Lucy Mae with a look that said, "See, I told you so!" Lucy Mae glared back. He was impossible.

Mr. Livingston, the boys' supervisor, and Miss Andrews, the girls' supervisor, organized the island kids. The girls stayed at the Shelter to knit quilt squares. Miss Andrews wanted to sew them together to make a quilt that could be raffled off at the Saturday dance. The money raised would be donated to the *Star* Fresh Air Fund. Lucy Mae rolled her eyes. She didn't mind helping the *Toronto Star* newspaper raise money for poor children to go to summer camp, but who wanted to knit on summer vacation?

CHAPTER 17
The Big Water Fight

THE BOYS FOLLOWED MR. LIVINGSTON TO the beach and paddled about while he organized a volleyball game. Jack nudged Dougie, who nudged back. Pretty soon the whole crew was horsing around in the water, disrupting the game. Mr. Livingston, in frustration, stopped the volleyball. "I guess we'll go swimming instead," he said. Young Jack Gordon always seemed able to set the agenda, the long-suffering supervisor thought to himself.

The crew took swimming far more seriously than volleyball. Sailors needed to know how to swim. The horseplay ended and Mr. Livingston heaved a sigh of relief.

After lunch, the crew met at the Shelter. Donnie had his baseball and glove, so Beans was sent to borrow a bat. The boys played around on the diamond for a bit, tossing the ball back and forth. A few more of the island kids joined them. Soon a full-scale game was underway. The girls brought their knitting to the bleachers. It was hot.

"Time out!" yelled one of the players. "I gotta take a leak." As he headed to the outdoor bathroom affectionately known as "The Cans," Jack made for the water fountain. Lucy Mae beat him to it.

"Hey! I was here first!"

Lucy Mae waggled her dark eyebrows at him. "Really?" she asked, as she flicked him with water.

Jack flicked her back. Lucy Mae grinned. Taking the quilt square she had just finished, she soaked it in the fountain. Slowly and deliberately, she squeezed it over Jack's head. Jack pulled off his ball cap. Filling it with water, he dumped it down Lucy Mae's back. It only took a minute before all the kids were in on it. Quilt squares and shirts became sponges, caps and shoes became buckets. But that wasn't enough.

Dougie ran home and got his mother's biggest cook pot. With that, he could completely douse his target. But the pot took a while to fill, causing a lineup at the fountain. Other sources of water were required. The kids who lived at the edge of the playing field obliged with garden hoses run onto the field, providing multiple sources of ammunition. Pretty soon, there were pots and pans and bailing buckets and washtubs scattered about the field, all filled with water. The kids were soaked. The field was soaked. Shoes came off and bare toes sunk into the rapidly forming mud puddles. Water was everywhere. But it still wasn't enough. Jack had an idea.

The Lawn Bowling Club was right across the street from the playing field. It was fenced to protect the greens, which had to be kept in pristine condition for the bowlers. The Club had a huge hose, the same size used by firemen, to water the greens. Launching himself over the fence into the Club grounds, Jack attached the hose to the water tank and opened the spigot. The water pressure surprised him; the hose leapt out of his hands and snaked across the greens as if it was possessed. Jack jumped to the rescue, dashing about the green after the hose. After a minute's hesitation, Donnie and Dougie leapt the fence and scrambled about the greens trying to help.

"Got it!" Jack finally yelled, as water continued to gush out of the hose. Then he looked up.

From the other side of the fence, the island constable was glaring at him. The rest of the kids were standing stock-still on the muddy field, watching.

"I guess the water fight is over, eh?" asked Jack, flashing his famous grin.

"Turn. That. Off."

Jack turned the spigot off.

"Now the water fight is over," said the constable grimly.

CHAPTER 18
Departure Day
Detroit, Michigan
Tuesday

"MOM, AREN'T YOU READY *YET?*"
"Henry, give me a bit of peace, PLEASE!" said Henry's mother with exasperation. "I have to decide what to pack."

"Take everything, Mom. I told you, the *Norey* needs a lot of weight so she won't get tippy. Pack the kitchen sink! Pack the piano! We don't want to get stuck!"

Mrs. Addison shut her eyes and tried to pretend that her son was somewhere else. Of course she loved him; she was his mother. But ever since he had started studying up on the steamboats of the Great Lakes, he had become an intolerable know-it-all. Not a moment went by that Henry didn't feel the need to share some earth-shattering tidbit about boilers or screws or trim or wheelhouses. Mrs. Addison couldn't be less interested in the workings of the engine room. She was far more concerned with the appropriate attire for the Grand Dining Hall.

"Henry!" she called. "Did you pack your costume for the Gala Ball?"

"Yup!" Henry riffled through the box from the costume rental place. "I've got it all – leather boots, pantaloons, jacket, vest, shirt, cutlass, eye patch and pirate hat. Does the shirt have to have ruffles, Mom?"

"If you want to be an authentic pirate for the Gala it does," Mrs. Addison replied. "Get it all in your bag, and fold it neatly. We're almost ready," she announced with an exhausted sigh.

"Mom, did you know that once there really was a pirate on Lake Ontario? His name was Bill Johnston and he had a hideout on a little island called Devil's Oven and…"

"Enough!" cried his mother. "Your father has hired a taxi to take us down to the port. Take your bag to the front door and watch for it."

Henry was beside himself with excitement. Without letting on to his parents, Henry had bicycled down to the docks on Saturday, Sunday and Monday. He got to know the route really well. He never wobbled on his bike any more. It always felt like a grand adventure, and sometimes he wished that he could share it with someone. But whenever he started thinking like that, he quickly reminded himself that all the other kids were morons. After all, they had accused him of lying about the new Ford station wagon, just as he knew they would. They didn't deserve to share his adventure.

Moses was pretty neat, though. Twice they ran into each other as Henry prowled the piers. On Monday Moses even had a fifteen-minute break, and he treated them both to a Popsicle and told Henry all kinds of interesting stuff about life down at the docks. Some of it Henry passed on to his parents, but he was careful to make it sound like it came from a library book. Moses was just as good as a book, after all. Better. But Henry knew his parents wouldn't approve of him going to the docks to visit Moses.

On every trip to the docks, Henry searched for the *Noronic*. But not once had he seen her. Moses said she put in at another dock. Henry just knew that she would be grander than any boat he had yet seen. Where was that taxi?

CHAPTER 19
Welcome to the SS Noronic

S HE WAS AMAZING.

Henry stared up at the massive superstructure of the *SS Noronic*. The gleaming black hull filled his vision, and he had to crane his neck to even see the three white decks that floated high above the water. The wheelhouse rose above that and Henry was sure he caught a glimpse of the captain surveying his boat through the wheelhouse window. Never in his secret visits to the freight dockyards had he ventured this close to a laker, been within touching distance of the massive chains that bound her to land, been allowed access to the gangplank that led to the mysterious and exciting world on board. Henry quivered with excitement.

While his father paid the taxi driver and tried to find a porter for their baggage, Henry looked this way and that, trying to take in all the sights and sounds at once. A band played near the gangplank to welcome the passengers. Colourful pennants strung in lines fore and aft snapped briskly in the wind. Passengers already aboard leaned over the rails high above him, waving white handkerchiefs in a farewell salute.

"Come on, Dad, hurry up!" cried Henry. "We gotta get on — we gotta get on RIGHT now!" Henry danced from foot to foot anxiously.

"Calm down, Henry," admonished his mother, adjusting her white gloves. "We're here in plenty of time. Be patient."

Be patient? He'd been waiting forever for this! For days, anyway.

Finally a porter arrived to load their various bags onto a rolling cart. Off he went towards another entry to the boat, low to the waterline. This gangway was much busier than the passenger gangway; dockhands and crew ran up and down the bouncy plank, loading last-minute items. Henry spared them hardly a glance as he grabbed his mother's hand and tried to hurry her to the boat.

Walking the "E" Deck gangplank gave Henry a funny feeling. It bounced up and down, just a little, and swayed back and forth at the same time. It was maybe just a little scary. After all, they were climbing very high, and there was nothing below them but cold water.

Once at the top, Henry and his parents stepped into another world. They were met by a tall, slim man dressed in a white uniform.

"Good morning to you, and welcome to the *Noronic*," the man said with a smile, reaching out to shake Mr. Addison's hand. "I'm First Officer Gerald Wood." He turned to a young man standing beside him. "This is Eddy, one of our busboys. He will take you to your stateroom and get you settled. Have a nice trip!"

The Addisons followed Eddy down a hallway. After all the activity outside, the hallway was nearly silent, all sound deadened by the thick carpeting beneath their feet and the luxurious draperies over the portholes. The walls were panelled in Canadian ash.

"Mom," Henry whispered, "it smells like our living room after you use the lemon oil." And so it did. Clearly many hands spent hours rubbing oil into the wood panelling to make it gleam. Henry felt like he was in a museum.

Eddy led them up two flights of beautiful curving stairs. The railings were rubbed smooth. "Hold on when you take the stairs," he warned them. "Once we're underway, the boat sometimes rolls when you don't expect it." Henry thought about what Moses had said.

"Do you have enough pig iron in the hold?" he whispered to Eddy. "My mom won't like it if it rolls."

Eddy smiled, and whispered back. "We've got all the pig iron we need. How'd you know about that anyway?"

Henry smiled. "I know lots of stuff about this boat," he said loudly. "I'm an expert."

"Is that so?" laughed Eddy. "Maybe you can teach me a few things, then. Your stateroom is on 'C' Deck," Eddy explained to Mr. and Mrs. Addison. "You entered the boat on 'E' Deck. That's the only deck that has a gangplank to get you on or off the boat. There's a map in your stateroom; it won't be long before you have a sense of where everything is. If you have any questions or feel lost, just find one of the crew members. We can all help you."

Eddy took a long metal key from his pocket and opened a panelled door. "Here is your home for the next week." With a flourish, he presented the key to Mr. Addison. "Welcome to the *Noronic.*"

CHAPTER 20
And the Band Played

THE MINUTE THE ADDISONS WERE ALONE IN their stateroom, Henry started to explore. There were twin beds for his mother and father, both with quilts his mother proclaimed "quite lovely." But no bed for Henry. In dismay, he turned to his father, who unlatched a berth that swung down from the wall.

"Oh boy!" shouted Henry, lying down for three seconds. Then he was up again, and into their private bathroom. "We've got a whole bathtub!" he shouted to his parents. But after that, there was nothing more to see. Nice as it was, it was really just a bedroom.

Henry wanted to explore the rest of the boat. His mother wanted to unpack and fix her makeup and take a nap and all kinds of other silly stuff. So Henry did what he always did in such situations: he set out to annoy his parents so much they would send him away. He was very good at it. In no time at all his mother tired of his whining and told him to go see the rest of the boat, just as if it were her idea. Henry bolted for the door.

"You absolutely cannot leave this boat!" his mother called after him. "Try to find some other children to play with!"

Henry didn't need other children. He wanted to play with the *Noronic*. Making his way down the hallway, Henry came to a big social hall. There were card tables set up at one end, and big comfy chairs scattered about. At one end was a long oak bar. A steward with a white coat stood behind it polishing glassware.

"Hey kid," called the steward. "Would you like a soda?"

Henry shrugged. "I don't have any money with me right now."

"You don't need money here, kid," replied the steward. "What kind do you like?"

Clutching a grape soda, Henry climbed another set of stairs to "B" Deck. He looked around in wonder. The whole forward half of the deck was one big ball-room. There was a little stage at one end, for a band, Henry thought. Turning to look aft, he saw a beautiful set of carved oak doors. Henry pushed one of the doors open just a crack. On the other side of the doorway was the dining room. All the tables had white tablecloths and they were set with fancy china and crystal and real flowers, just like his dad had said. Henry couldn't believe his eyes. Boy, was his mom ever going to like it here!

Henry himself was more interested in the huge picture windows on all sides of the dining room. Through the glass, Henry could see lots of passengers gathering on the outside deck. That's where he wanted to be.

Leaning over the rail on "B" Deck, Henry felt like he could see the whole world. Just below him, passengers on "C" Deck were also clustered at the rail. Above him, the "A" Deck passengers waved hankies. The band on the dock was so far below him it looked like it was a million miles away. The "E" Deck gangplank was lifted away. The crew entry was closed and sealed. The passengers started to cheer.

"Goodbye! Goodbye!" they all shouted, frantically waving their hankies. Henry, as usual, had forgotten his. In his excitement he raised his grape soda high into the air and waved just as frantically as everyone else. "Goodbye!" he shouted, to no one in particular. "Goodbye!"

Grape soda fizzed out of the bottle, spattering his white-collared shirt and navy blue tie and dripping onto the "C" Deck passengers. Nobody noticed. Black smoke poured from the smokestack, tiny men on the dock loosened the final ropes and the *Noronic* was free. The boat shivered as the engines came to life. Water churned far below Henry. The band played faster.

All of a sudden the band was drowned out by a strange sound. Deep, growly and shuddering, the steamship's distinctive whistle blew.

The *SS Noronic* was underway.

CHAPTER 21
Jack's Punishment
Toronto Islands
Wednesday

JACK STOOD AWKWARDLY OUTSIDE THE DOOR OF the Ward's Island Association Clubhouse, waiting to be called in. A meeting had been arranged to discuss the damage done to the lawn bowling greens. As usual, Jack was named the culprit and just as usual, he was prepared to take his punishment. But he didn't really see what was so bad. The greens would grow back, after all.

The crew had come in support. Sort of. Dougie was on a roll.

"They shouldn't be punishing you! It's only old fogies who use the bowling greens anyway, so what do they care if they're muddy? They can wear boots if they don't want their precious tootsies all mucky – it's only dirt. Jeez, this is stupid!" Jack threw him a smile, and looked to Donnie, his right-hand man.

"Whaddya want me to say, Jackie boy? You're my best bud! But you always take things one step too far and all of a sudden we're all in for it. My dad's making me and Dougie clean the shed. We have to miss Supervision till it's done. That stinks!"

"He's right," added Lucy Mae righteously. "We were having a lot of fun until you hopped the fence."

One of the dads opened the door and beckoned Jack in. As Jack stepped across the threshold, he turned back to his friends.

"Thanks a lot, guys," he said, hurt. Then he went inside.

The president of the Ward's Island Association and the chairman of the Lawn Bowling Committee were sitting at a table on the stage. That put Jack in an even lowlier position that he had expected. The tirade began and Jack tuned out. Just tell me my punishment and let's be done, he thought wearily. He looked around. His father was there, looking grim. That was to be expected; his father always looked grim when Jack was in trouble. Jack was more disconcerted to see Captain Clapp sitting on a bench at the back. If he regretted anything about the water fight, it was that it put his plan to impress the Captain back a step or two. But it could still work; he just had to win the Cup.

Jack heard the word "punishment" and tuned back in.

"The Lawn Bowling Committee will train you in the maintenance and upkeep of the greens. For the rest of the summer, that will be your job. You will not only repair the damage you've done, you will tend the grass as if it were the most precious piece of earth on the island. Do you understand?"

Jack nodded solemnly. It was just as he expected. He turned to go.

"There is one further punishment." Jack frowned, and turned to his father.

"I'm taking away your sailboat, Jack. You have to learn to think before you act. I don't know how to teach you that, except by making the punishment something that really matters. There will be no discussion. *Frosty Friday* is beached until further notice."

Jack stared at his father in horror. He couldn't mean it. He couldn't.

CHAPTER 22
The Welland Canal
Lake Erie
Thursday

HENRY SAT IN A DECK CHAIR ON "B" DECK, waiting for his morning hot chocolate. Generally, the stewards served hot soup in the morning to the passengers out on deck, but Henry had made it clear on the very first day of the cruise that he wasn't fond of soup. So he got hot chocolate. Henry thought shipboard life was just swell.

The best part was that his parents let him roam around all day without supervision. They figured he had found some other children to play with. Little did they know that he spent the hours down in the engine room with Mr. Bonnell, the chief engineer, or tagging after Eddy, the busboy. The workings of the ship were fascinating; a thirteen-year-old boy could hardly be expected to be interested in games like euchre or bingo. But he had to admit that the Gala Masquerade Dinner had been fun. Henry's pirate costume had won him a prize.

Today was going to be the best day of all. Henry had laid claim to a prime seat on deck right after breakfast so that he wouldn't miss anything. Today the *Noronic* would pass through the locks of the Welland Canal. He could hardly wait.

To get to Toronto, the *Noronic* had to pass from Lake Erie into Lake Ontario. But there was a problem. Lake Erie was 326 feet higher than Lake Ontario. The only natural waterway between the lakes was the Niagara River, and a boat using the river would have had to go over Niagara Falls to get down into Lake Ontario. So more than a hundred years earlier, a canal had been built to join the lakes so that the big lakers could pass from one to the other. Mr. Addison said that it was a very important canal because through it went the boats that carried the steel to the Ford plant to build the Dream Wagons.

But the canal had the same problem as the river; Lake Erie was still 326 feet higher than Lake Ontario. So the engineers added a series of locks to lift the boats into Lake Erie. The locks were like little compartments in the canal that could be filled with water. When the water rose, the boats rose. If the water was drained, the boats lowered. The Welland Canal was like a staircase for ships.

Chief Engineer Bonnell told Henry that in the old days, the boats were pulled through the canals by oxen that walked along on the towpath beside the canal. Nowadays, boats could go through under their own power. The engineer told Henry to watch his fingers if he was outside, because sometimes the *Noronic* was almost as wide as the lock itself, leaving just inches to spare between the boat and the canal wall.

Entering the canal at Port Colborne, Henry wondered what the engineer was on about. The canal was huge! As wide as the biggest river he'd ever seen. But in no time at all, the waterway narrowed. The concrete walls on either side of the canal closed in on Henry. He started to worry; even with the engineer's warning, Henry hadn't been prepared for this. Was the *Noronic* going to fit?

Slowly, slowly, the *Noronic* came to a stop just before she hit the forward gates of the first lock. At the stern of the ship, Henry could see the gates behind the boat creak to a close. Men on both shores secured ropes from the boat to the bollards. The *Noronic* was locked in.

Henry dashed to the bow. From "B" Deck, he could look over the gates to see what was ahead. There was nothing there. Henry raced up to "A" Deck. With the added height, Henry could see water. But so far below him; surely the *Noronic* couldn't sink that low!

As he watched, water began to pour out of the lock. Swirling, churning, it rushed through the valves into the next compartment. Henry could feel the boat sinking, sinking, sinking. The concrete walls of the lock rose up on both sides. Henry reached out and touched the slime. They were so close. It was almost terrifying. Then the water stopped.

The front gates started to open. Henry shut his eyes. Would the *Noronic* fall over the precipice? But magically, it seemed, the water in the two compartments had evened out. The steam whistle growled in its odd voice as the *Noronic* made her way forward into the next compartment. There were seven locks to go. By then, the boat would be 326 feet lower and ready to enter Lake Ontario.

Next stop – Pier Nine, Toronto, Ontario.

CHAPTER 23
A Million Tiny Pieces
The Eastern Gap
Friday

STANDING ON THE SHORE WITH CHARLIE AND Lucy, Jack watched his friends practice in the Cove without him. It was nearly killing him. He knew he was being unreasonable, but he wished they'd stopped sailing too. By the time the Cup came, they'd be better than him. Not that it mattered; he probably wouldn't even be allowed to try for the Cup. All Donnie and Dougie had to do was miss Supervision for a couple of days. That was nothing.

In his heart, though, Jack knew that he was the only one who should be punished, not the crew. Nobody told him to climb the fence. He hadn't meant to wreck the greens, though. Losing *Frosty Friday* was pretty harsh when it was just an accident.

He couldn't stand watching anymore. Jack left the Cove. He thought about going to see the Captain, but was too ashamed. The Captain hadn't spoken to him that day in the clubhouse, nor had he spoken to him since. It looked like he'd been right all along. Jack was a troublemaker. A bad influence. Always would be. No "captain" qualities in that Jackie character, no siree.

Jack wandered home. His mom smiled sympathetically, but that didn't help. On top of everything he was lonely, with the crew busy preparing for the race. Jack grabbed his cigar box and took it to the Eastern Gap. Sitting down on the concrete breakwater that stopped the waters of the Gap from washing away any more of Ward's Island, Jack dangled his legs over the water. He'd never be a laker captain.

Jack opened the cigar box. The first thing he took out was a photo of the *Cayuga*. For a long time, the *Cayuga* had been his favourite boat. After all, she was in Toronto Harbour all the time and she was a really pretty boat. Sleek. But she was small. Jack had wanted something grander. He stared at the photograph. Clearly, he didn't need it any more. Slowly and deliberately, Jack tore the photo into a million tiny pieces and let them flutter into the wind. They danced about for a moment, then dropped to the water. Then they sank.

Next up was the *Wyandotte*. She was built in 1908, a freighter. Jack had torn this page out of *The Shipping*

News because the *Wyandotte* was the first laker to have self-loading equipment. Back when he thought he'd be a captain, he'd wanted to have a boat with the most up-to-date equipment like the *Wyandotte* had in her day. No matter now. Pieces of the *Wyandotte* followed the *Cayuga* into the Gap. Page after page, boat after boat followed. One by one, his dreams sank to the bottom.

Finally Jack reached into his pocket. The only page left was his *Noronic* advertisement. If Jack hadn't been well practiced at taking his punishment like a man, he'd have felt like blubbering. The *Noronic* was supposed to be his. All seven thousand tons of her. Without *Frosty Friday*, he couldn't win the Cup. Without the Cup, the Captain wouldn't see his good qualities. Without the Captain to vouch for him, he'd never get on a training ship, Jack was sure of it. All the pieces fit. Badly.

Jack tore up the ad and threw the pieces into the Gap.

A low growl rolled over the lake. Jack looked up, alert. Was it thunder? But there wasn't a cloud in the sky. It sounded again. It was a ship, Jack thought. With a very odd whistle. Jack peered down the Gap into the lake, squinting into the sun. Finally he saw it.

One smokestack. A crow's nest silhouetted against the blue sky. An odd whistle. It had to be the *Noronic*. Jack stood up and stared with all his might. He waited as the great ship sailed closer. It was the *Noronic* all right. Jack was quivering as he stood on the breakwater.

Majestically the *Noronic* entered the Eastern Gap. Her whistle sounded and Jack had to cover his ears. She cruised right past him. So close, he could see the passengers through the big picture windows. Her pennants whipped in the breeze. Jack was frozen.

High above him, a small, thin boy in a suit was staring out through the picture window. Jack saw him. Still somewhat mesmerized, Jack raised his hand and tentatively gave a wave. He could see the boy frown, and then squint.

Jack waved again, harder.

CHAPTER 24
The Queen Arrives
The Eastern Gap

HENRY HAD BEEN TOYING WITH HIS DINNER in bored fashion. His parents were discussing what to do when they docked in Toronto. Mrs. Addison just couldn't decide.

"The purser said that *Gone with the Wind* is playing at the Odeon. Wouldn't that be lovely? But then, he also said that *Yessir, That's My Baby!* is at the Uptown. Oh, I just love Donald O'Connor!" she said dreamily. Henry and his dad rolled their eyes. "I just don't know!"

At that moment, the *Noronic's* whistle began to quiver and rumble. Henry thought they were probably close to docking.

After more debate, it was decided that they would see *Gone with the Wind*. Apparently there was a scene in the movie with a great fire, and his mother thought it would be quite exciting to watch.

"Dad," Henry whispered, "it's a *love* story. Do I have to come?"

Mr. Addison sighed. "Dear, if Henry promises to stay on board, could he stay behind? The movie won't interest him, and you'll enjoy it more knowing he's having a good time."

"Will you be all right?" asked his mother dubiously.

"Sure!" said Henry. "I'll stay with Eddy."

To Henry's great relief, it was agreed. Love stories, yech! He attacked his dessert with enthusiasm so he could be excused from the table to see the boat dock. As he ate, Henry glanced out the big picture window. He could see a shoreline, and way below him, some kind of a breakwater with a boy standing on it. The boy was waving.

The *Noronic* was passing through the Eastern Gap. On one side the skyline of Toronto was coming into sight. On the other side was Ward's Island, the most easterly bit of the Toronto Islands. The islands formed the south side of the harbour, sheltering the city from storms and waves. Eddy said they were pretty swell, with parks and beaches and stuff. Some people even lived there.

Henry looked curiously at the Gap. It was narrow; it reminded him of the Welland Canal. There was a low concrete wall on either side of the *Noronic,* holding the land back so the *Noronic* could pass through. On the other side of the Gap lay the open harbour and Pier Nine. Way below him on the break-water was that boy, still waving.

Henry waved back. He felt like a king, waving to his subject.

CHAPTER 25
The Race to Pier Nine

J ACK STOOD DUMBFOUNDED. HE KNEW SHE'D BE big, but wow! Dropping his empty cigar box, Jack raced for the Cove to tell the crew.

But they already knew. The *Noronic* had cruised right through the middle of their practice race, scattering the tiny prams as if they were nothing more than flotsam and jetsam. Safe out of the way, the sailors steered into the wind to let their sails luff and just sat, sails flapping idly, watching the spectacle.

"Does Jack know?" called Donnie to the others. "We gotta tell Jack!"

Just as the words left his mouth, they saw Jack running along the shore of Clapp's Cove, shouting and waving.

"Jack knows!" laughed Dougie, and the crew turned their sails for home. Jack helped them drag their prams on shore.

"We gotta get over there for a closer look, right away," said Jack, who was more agitated than the crew had ever seen him.

"Why don't we take the boats?" asked Beans. "They're already in the water."

Jack groaned. "I can't."

"We can't either," piped up Lucy Mae. "Charles and I haven't got a boat." Jack threw a look her way gratefully.

Donnie took charge. "You can come with us," he said decisively. "Nobody said you couldn't *ride* in a boat, Jack, just that you couldn't sail *Frosty Friday*. You ride with Beans, I'll take Lucy and Dougie will take Charlie. Let's go, everybody!"

Jack hesitated a moment. He wasn't sure he could be just a passenger. But it was the fastest way to the *Noronic*. Jack sighed, then he pushed Beans's pram back into the water and hopped in. He kneeled in the bow to stabilize the boat, then squeezed his lips together, trying to stop any orders from coming out of it. He wasn't the captain here.

The tiny fleet tacked their way across the harbour, following in the *Noronic's* wake. They watched from behind as the great boat eased her nose into Pier Nine. They heard the steam engines shut down. The black smoke that had been pouring out of the smokestack began to dissipate in the clear evening air. They saw the first lines thrown from the bow to the waiting dockworkers on the pier.

Following Donnie's lead, the trio of prams came up alongside the ferry dock next to Pier Nine. It wasn't really public docking, but everybody knew the island kids' prams so they'd be safe there. They tied their boats to the cleats, hopped out of them and started to run towards Pier Nine. In his haste to get there, Jack almost didn't see his father, who was preparing to board the return ferry after his day of work in the city.

"Jack!" Mr. Gordon shouted. "Just where do you think you're going? It's dinnertime!"

Jack was caught wrong-footed. As usual, he hadn't thought first. None of the crew had. It was five-thirty and all the moms would be expecting them home. Jack turned a penitent face towards his father.

"Please, Dad, please let me stay. The *Noronic* just docked. I've never had a chance to see her. Captain says she only comes once a year and she only stays one night. I didn't take *Frosty Friday* – I didn't break the rules. Please?"

For all Mr. Gordon's sternness, he was not completely unaware of his son's dreams. "Stay together, and be back by dark. Who's with you?" The rest of the crew poked their heads around the corner of the ferry building. "Why am I not surprised?" Mr. Gordon sighed. "All right, I give ALL of you permission, and I'll tell your mothers. But Jack, next time…" Mr. Gordon's eyebrows lifted and he regarded Jack very seriously. "Next time, THINK AHEAD."

"Thanks, Dad!" The crew raced off towards Pier Nine, with Jack in the lead. Jack had his grin back. He might never get to be a captain, but at least he could see his dream ship.

CHAPTER 26
The Boy in the Necktie

Henry waved to his parents from "C" Deck. Boy, was he glad he didn't have to go to the movie. He set out to find Eddy.

As usual, Eddy was in the dining room, cleaning up after the second sitting. Henry plunked himself down in one of the empty chairs.

"Hey, Eddy," said Henry.

"Whatcha doin', kid?" asked Eddy.

"Staying with you. My folks left me on board while they went to the movies," replied Henry.

"Now, that's too bad," said Eddy, "because once I'm done here, I'm off for a couple of hours. I'm going ashore for a bit of fun. But I'll be back later. I have to clean up the bar after everyone's bedded down for the night."

"Oh," said Henry. "Eddy, do you know there's a curse on this boat?"

"Where did ya hear that, kid?"

"Just around. Is it true?"

"Some say so. Myself, I don't hold with that nonsense," said Eddy. "And no one really has the story right anyway. Some people think the curse was on the boat, some say it was on the captain.

"And if it was on the captain," he mused, "it wouldn't matter much, now would it? We've got a different captain now. Done!" Eddy wiped the last table with a flourish. "Be good, kid."

And Eddy was off.

Now what? Henry climbed out on "A" Deck to take a look at the view. Pier Nine was bustling with activity. Passengers were making their way down the "E" Deck gangplank, off to the many entertainments in the city. Other passengers were meeting friends on the pier and bringing them on board as guests. Trucks were pulling up with supplies to be loaded on board. Onlookers wandered the pier, admiring the boats.

The *Noronic* was not the only boat moored at Pier Nine. In the next slip lay the *Cayuga*. Her engines were running, smoke was pouring out of her smokestacks, and hordes of sightseers were climbing aboard for her evening cruise. The *Cayuga* was smaller than the *Noronic*, but Henry still thought she had fine lines. At least, that was what Eddy said. Lots of couples were boarding; it must be a romantic dinner cruise or something. Henry sniffed in disdain. It was fun to watch her pull out, though.

In the slip on the other side of the *Noronic* lay the *Kingston*. She was an old boat. Eddy said that she was leaving the next morning on her final cruise ever. Henry wondered what they did with old boats.

For a while, Henry watched the ferry boats that plied back and forth across the harbour between the city and the islands. Compared to the *Noronic*, they looked so small. And the sailboats – scattered about the harbour there seemed to be hundreds of fluffy white sails. A little group of three boats caught Henry's eye. It was a small flotilla of silly looking sailboats. Henry watched them curiously.

They were making their way towards the *Noronic*. Henry hoped they knew what they were doing, because if they didn't, the little boats were all about to crash right into "E" Deck.

He raced down to "C" Deck for a better view. By the time he got there, the flotilla had landed alongside Pier Nine near the ferry dock and the tiny boats were neatly tied to the cleats in the pier.

Squinting against the late afternoon sun, Henry stared at the sailors. They were all kids! Kids like him. And they had their own sailboats; there weren't any grown-ups with them. Henry was impressed. One tall, skinny, blond boy, who was talking to an older man, looked like the leader of the group. And he kind of looked like the boy on the breakwater; the one that waved. If he was, that blond boy had made it across the harbour nearly as quickly as the *Noronic*.

The kids must have sailed over to get a closer look at his boat. Henry felt proud. His boat was so much bigger than theirs. He watched as the group wandered up and down the length of Pier Nine, examining the *Noronic*. The blond kid looked like he was talking a mile a minute. Henry watched them for awhile then went back inside to get another soda.

The crew had covered every inch of the port side of the *Noronic*. But that was all they could do. Jack was itching to get aboard. There was only one gangplank, which was too bad – if there had been two they might have been able to sneak aboard. Jack watched the "E" Deck gangplank, looking for an opportunity. Lots of passengers were getting off to go into the city, but a fair few people were getting on, too. Most of them were met at the top of the gangplank by friends; there was a lot of hugging and kissing and that "It's so nice to see you!" kind of stuff. Obviously it was okay to go on the ship if you knew somebody. But Jack didn't know anybody.

He looked up to the passenger decks, and saw a kid about his own age leaning over the rail, holding a soda. It kind of looked like the kid who had waved to him. Jack had an idea. He cupped his hands around his mouth and yelled.

"Hey, you! In the necktie! Hi!"

Henry started. *He* was wearing a necktie. He looked over the rail.

"Down here!" Henry looked down. Six heads were looking up at him.

"We like your boat!" called out the blond boy.

"Yeah, it's swell!" shouted back Henry.

"Can we come on board? Can you show us around?"

Henry was astounded. Bring those kids on board? As his guests? He knew it was allowed because he had seen other passengers do it, but they were grown-ups. His parents would kill him.

"Please? We won't stay long. We just want to see inside."

On the other hand, his parents had only told him not to get *off* the boat. They hadn't said anything about bringing people *on*. The way those kids were dressed, they'd probably never get a chance to be real passengers, on the *Noronic* or any other boat. Henry bit his lip. He was pretty much an expert on the *Noronic*. He could certainly tell them a thing or two.

"Meet me at the gangplank!" he yelled down, wondering what on earth he was getting himself into.

CHAPTER 27
Sharing the Curse

THE ISLAND KIDS NEEDED NO SECOND invitation. They hurried to the "E" Deck gangplank and waited for Henry to come to clear their passage with the crew. Once they were inside, Henry led them into the long quiet hallway. The boys surreptitiously checked the bottom of their boat shoes for duck muck. Lucy Mae looked around in wonder.

Henry stuck his hand out in Jack's direction. "I'm Henry, from Detroit."

Jack looked at the hand oddly. Kids didn't shake hands. "I'm Jack. These here are the guys, my crew. We live on Ward's Island — you passed it coming in."

"And I'm Lucy Mae," piped in Lucy, glaring at Jack. "I live on the island too. This is really nice."

The group stood awkwardly. Henry didn't have a lot of experience with kids his own age, and the island kids — well, for all their tattered clothes, they looked so sure of themselves. Henry reminded himself that this was his party; he was the one who belonged here. "Have you ever been on a laker before?"

The islanders shook their heads, although Jack was quick to add, "But we know all about them. There's a laker captain that lives on the island and he taught us about the boats and about the lakes. He taught us to sail. I'm training to be a captain one day. Maybe I'll even captain this boat."

Even with the loss of *Frosty Friday* still smarting, Jack couldn't help showing off just a bit. He didn't want to let Henry see how excited he was to be on the *Noronic.*

Henry established his own credentials. "I'm a car man myself. I'm from Detroit, after all. But I've been on this old tub for a while now, so I know her pretty good. Did you know there's a curse on her?"

Henry had them. When you're fourteen, a curse trumps all other stories. Taking command, Henry led them down the hallway to his stateroom and ushered them in with a flourish. The island kids spent a minute or two examining the room then got comfortable on the two beds.

"Spill!" demanded Jack.

Henry climbed onto his bunk and looked down

into six attentive faces. "I rode my bike down to the docks," he began. "No kids are allowed, and a huge man chased me down, captured me and took my bike away."

Henry's story grew and grew. By the time he was done, it was amazing that the curse hadn't caused the *Noronic* to sink to the bottom a hundred times over. Jack was skeptical.

"Captain Clapp says that the *Noronic* has never lost a man," he said thoughtfully. "That it's a lucky boat."

"It is," replied Henry. "But," he added, more ominously, "Moses says there are two kinds of luck. And you never know which one you're going to get."

Lucy Mae's eyes were sparkling. "That was a great story!" she exclaimed. "May we see the ballroom now?"

"No, the engine room!" the boys shouted her down.

Henry made the decision. "We'll start at the bottom," he decreed, "and make our way up to the top."

The group trooped out of the Addisons' stateroom, following Henry down to "E" Deck. "Down here, we got the engine room, the cargo hold and the crew quarters. And this is where you get on and off the boat. There aren't any gangplanks on the upper decks," Henry explained.

"Hey, Mr. Bonnell, these guys want to see the engine. Can we come in?" Henry shouted into the engine room. Jack was immediately serious. This was it. The heart and soul of a seven-thousand-ton laker. The biggest passenger cruiser on the Great Lakes. The Queen of the Inland Seas. He was finally here.

Mr. Bonnell gave them a quick tour, then Henry led the crew out. Jack wanted to stay in the engine room, but the crew wanted to see the rest of the ship. They trooped up to "D" Deck, wandering another long, carpeted hallway past numerous beautifully oiled stateroom doors, then climbed the curving staircase to "B" Deck. For Lucy Mae, this was the heart of the ship. The great picture windows, the ballroom and the dining room left her in awe.

"You are so lucky, Henry!" she breathed. "I would love to live here!"

Henry straightened with pride. "Anybody thirsty?" he asked grandly. "Let's go to the bar."

With so many passengers ashore, there was lots of room for all of them to sit at the polished oak bar and have a soda. As they drank, the crew kept Henry entertained with tales of island life. For some reason, they seemed to concentrate on Jack's exploits – the ones that regularly got them all into trouble. They laughed a lot. Henry listened carefully. Their lives were so different from his. More interesting, that was for sure. It was hard to stop from thinking that he'd rather be an island kid.

As the crew told stories, Jack looked around the social hall. A few people were playing cards, others just talking. As captain, he would not only be responsible for the ship, but for all the people too. He would eat dinner with them in the dining room, and chat with them in the lounge. He knew he could do it. He closed his eyes. But he'd probably never get the chance.

CHAPTER 28
The Thank-You Gift

AFTER THE CREW FINISHED THEIR SODAS, Jack had an idea. "Hey, Henry, this has been great. Now, we'll do *you* a favour. Want to come for a sail?"

Henry caught his breath. In those tiny little boats? With no grown-ups around? Jack talked a good game, but Henry wondered if he really knew what he was doing.

"C'mon, Henry," said Dougie. "This big tub keeps you too far away from the water. You gotta get close to the wind and the waves. It'll be fun."

"I can't," stammered Henry, "but thanks. My parents went to the movies and I'm not allowed to leave the ship."

"What movie?" asked Jack briskly.

"Some romance. Icky stuff. There's a fire."

"That'll probably be *Gone with the Wind*. My mom went to see it too. It's the longest movie in history. We've got lots of time." Jack started down the stairs towards the "E" Deck gangplank. "Come on!"

Henry didn't feel that he had any choice in the matter. Jack was like a force of nature. Henry had never met anyone like him. He followed the crew to the three little prams tied up at the ferry dock. Jack looked around in dismay for *Frosty Friday*. He had completely forgotten that he didn't have a boat to offer. As usual, he had acted without thinking. Now what?

Donnie jumped into the breach. "Here's my boat, Henry," he said. "Get in." The crew helped him climb into Donnie's boat. Then they looked at one another. There was only room for two in each boat. Somebody would have to stay behind.

"I'd really like to stay close to the *Noronic* a bit longer," said Jack. "Make sure you give Henry our super-deluxe tour."

"You sure, Jack?" asked Beans quietly. "You can take my boat. We won't tell your dad."

"Absolutely," replied Jack firmly. "Remember — the super-deluxe!"

In moments the prams were untied and bobbing free on the waves. Each of the captains found their wind, and one by one the boats began to move across the water. Henry's face had a tight look. Jack was pretty sure he'd lose it soon. It was impossible, in Jack's opinion, not to enjoy flying over the water. It was the greatest gift he had to share and it was his duty to thank Henry for the *Noronic* the best way he knew.

Standing alone on the pier as the crew did his duty was the hardest thing Jack had ever done.

THE PRAMS TACKED ACROSS THE HARBOUR and sailed close in to Ward's Island, close enough to point out their cottages to Henry. They held to at the mouth of the Eastern Gap while they watched a freighter steam through. They darted in and out around the island ferries, annoying the ferry captains enough to toot their horns and yell, "Get out of here!" Henry had thought the ferries looked so small from the "A" Deck of the *Noronic,* but bearing down on an eight-foot pram those same ferries were terrifyingly large.

By the time Henry disembarked at Pier Nine, he had definitely lost that tight look. "That was fantastic!" Henry grinned. "Just super! Thanks, guys!" Henry pumped Donnie's hand. Then he shook Beans's hand, then Dougie's. He said goodbye to Lucy Mae. Last of all, he went to Jack.

"Sorry you couldn't come. That was a great idea you had and I'll never forget it, Jack. Thanks." Henry solemnly shook Jack's hand too.

Back on board, Henry raced up to the outside promenade of "C" Deck to watch the Cove Fleet head back to the island. He was exhilarated. It had been an evening like none other. So much better than a movie.

CHAPTER 29
The Famous Whistle
Very Late Friday Night

JACK WAS THOUGHTFUL ON THE WAY BACK TO the island. He'd seen the *Noronic*. His dream had taken shape and form, even if it was never going to happen. But that night Jack couldn't sleep. In his mind, he went over every inch of the boat, setting it into his memory so he wouldn't forget. She was a fine lady, the *SS Noronic*.

Henry couldn't sleep either. He couldn't share his adventure with his parents or he'd be in big trouble, but he wanted to tell somebody about the Cove Fleet. He'd really liked the island kids. They were different from the kids at his school. And much as he had lorded it over them, just a little bit, they'd given him new appreciation for the *Norey*. He was amazed that they could be so interested without ever having seen her.

Henry shrugged. Must be because they lived on an island. They wore shorts and t-shirts instead of collared shirts and suspenders. They didn't much worry about rules. They were too busy having fun. Henry wished he could visit them on Ward's Island some day. Maybe next summer he would tell his dad that they should go to the island for their vacation.

It was a lovely evening in Toronto, so Jack and Henry weren't the only ones awake. The *Cayuga* had just returned to Pier Nine after her evening cruise; passengers were making their way back to their cars to go home. Couples were strolling along the water's edge, hand in hand, enjoying the lights of the boats and the warm breeze. Ross Leitch's water taxi was cruising about the dock, just in case one of the islanders wanted to pay for a late-night lift home.

On the *Noronic*, a few card parties were still in full swing although the orchestra had long since packed up. Eddy was back, and he and a few other bellboys were doing a final cleanup after the dance. The job was taking a long time as many of the crew members, including the captain, had taken shore leave that night, leaving all the work for a very few. But by 2:30 a.m., most of the passengers and many of the crew had made their way back to the boat and were settling in for the night.

ONE OF THE PASSENGERS on "C" Deck was making his way back to his stateroom to go to bed when he smelled something odd. The man frowned, and sniffed once or twice. He knew that smell. Smoke.

The man followed his nose to the end of the hallway. There was a haze around the door of the linen closet, where the extra sheets and towels were kept. He tried the door, but it was locked, so he found a bellboy who had a key and together they opened it. Smoke poured out. Peering through it, the men could see an orange glow; the sheets were smouldering. The bellboy ran to get a fire extinguisher.

By the time he got back, there were flickers of flame deep within the closet. The extinguisher didn't help. Throwing it aside, the two men ran down the hallway to get the ship's firehose. They reeled it back to the linen closet and turned it on the growing flames. No water came out.

Both men could tell the fire was already out of control. The passenger left the bellboy and ran downstairs to wake his family, getting them off the ship in a hurry. He didn't wake anyone else.

The bellboy ran to the social hall to pull the fire alarm. It was designed to ring in the wheelhouse. From the wheelhouse, the officer on watch could pull a switch to sound the klaxon horns that would wake the passengers. But the wheelhouse was deserted. There was no one there to hear the alarm.

The bellboy ran down to "E" Deck and found the wheelsman. "Fire, sir! Fire portside on 'C' Deck!" He then continued along to the crew's quarters and woke the other bellboys. They grabbed some clothes and jumped on to the dock through an open freight door. They didn't wake the passengers either.

The wheelsman rushed from "E" Deck all the way up to "A" Deck and woke the First Officer. "Fire!" he yelled, pounding on the door.

The First Officer raced to the empty wheelhouse and pulled the switch. Finally the klaxon horns began to clang. He pulled the whistle cord to sound the SOS code to everyone within hearing. But the *Noronic*'s famous whistle jammed. The only sound that issued was a long mournful call, and it would not stop. It drowned out the klaxons. It drowned out the crackle of the flames. Ten precious minutes had passed since the fire had been discovered, and the passengers were only just beginning to realize that they were in mortal danger.

CHAPTER 30
Stealing the Shepherd

HENRY HEARD THE SHOUTING FIRST. HE HAD been half asleep, flying over the waves in Donnie's pram when the noise startled him awake. Curious, he hopped down from his bunk and opened the door. The corridor was filled with smoke. Henry slammed it shut, but not before he saw a woman go by, her nightgown on fire.

"Dad! Mom!" he shouted. "Wake up, something's wrong!" Henry danced from one foot to the other as his dad leapt from the bed. "What'll we do?"

Mr. Addison didn't open the door again. "I smell smoke," he said gravely. "There must be a fire on board. Quiet, everybody."

They all listened. Most of the shouting seemed to be coming from the stern of the ship. "Get your shoes," said Mr. Addison. "Don't worry about clothes. Be as quick as you can. Henry, go wet some washcloths from the bathroom. We'll tie them over our mouths and noses. When I open the door, we probably won't be able to see. We're going to turn left and go towards the bow of the ship. We'll hold hands, Henry in the middle. We'll get to the front of the ship, away from the fire. Everybody understand?"

Henry was shaking with fear. He held tight to his parents' hands.

"One, two, three," called his dad, "go!" Mr. Addison pulled open the door. The smoke hurt Henry's eyes and the heat was unbearable. Flames were licking along the highly oiled wood panelling in the corridor. Henry felt like he would explode. But his dad pulled him and his mother roughly along the hallway, pushing past screaming passengers in a determined line towards the bow of the *Noronic*. When they got there, the smoke was thinner. Henry pulled the washcloth off his face and looked down. They had made it away from the fire, but now were stuck two stories above the dock with no way down.

JACK STILL COULDN'T SLEEP. He couldn't get the *Noronic* out of his mind. He had to see her one more time before he could sleep. He hopped out of bed.

Still in his pajamas, Jack tiptoed out of the cottage, carefully shutting the screen door. Pulling on his boat shoes, he went round to the city side of the cottage to look for the *Noronic's* lights. Instead he saw flames, shooting over a hundred feet in the air. Jack's brain couldn't immediately register what he was seeing. He peered across the harbour, still looking for the *Noronic*. Finally he understood. The Queen was on fire.

Without thinking, Jack ran to Clapp's Cove. He pushed the *Shepherd* into the water and started the tiny motor. He didn't care who heard him. The *Noronic* needed help. Jack steered in a straight line directly towards the inferno. He couldn't believe what he was seeing. The closer he got, the worse it looked. All the upper decks were on fire, and he could see people silhouetted against the flames.

Was one of those people Henry?

As Jack neared the boat, the heat grew more and more intense. It looked like the boat was melting, it was so hot. Paint was peeling off the outside cabin walls; varnish seemed to be vapourizing from the wooden rails. The cabin window glass was melting. The hull was so hot the lake water was almost boiling around it. The *Noronic* was doomed. Jack heard a shout.

"Jack, what the hell are you doing?! Get away from here, it's dangerous!" It was Ross Leitch, calling from his water taxi. Jack was overwhelmed; getting away seemed like a very good idea. But before he could act, the *Shepherd* was nearly swamped by an object hurtling into the water in front of him. Jack grabbed the gunwales to steady the boat. The object popped back up, partially out of the water. It was a man. A man who had just plunged from seventy feet above him and whose hair had all been burnt off.

"Help me," he pleaded, reaching out towards Jack.

CHAPTER 31
Mortal Peril

B Y NOW, ALARMS HAD BEEN SENT THROUGH-out the city of Toronto and the dock was crowded with people. Police were trying to clear space for the fire rigs to get close. Water was pouring from the hoses onto the fire, but the ferocious heat turned the water to steam before it could do any good. So the firemen concentrated on getting passengers off the boat. They manoeuvred their tall ladders towards the highest decks where most of the people were trapped, and one by one, a few lucky individuals clambered down. But there weren't enough ladders.

Henry's dad scanned the dock. There were no good choices. Some passengers were jumping three or four stories down onto the concrete. Some were trying to get to the ladders, but the Addisons would have to go through the flames to do that. Quickly, Mr. Addison hoisted his wife up on the rail.

"See the rope there?" he asked her, pointing to the rope that tied the *Noronic* tight to the dock. "I want you to cross your legs over the rope. Don't worry, I'll hold you. Now let your body hang from the rope. I'll slide you over the rail, and you'll take the rope in both hands."

"I can't!" cried Mrs. Addison.

"You can!" her husband shouted back. "Gently now, hand over hand, walk yourself down the rope. Keep your legs wrapped around it. You can do it."

Slowly Mrs. Addison began to make her way down the rope, weeping the whole time. Several other passengers rushed over and pushed Henry and his dad away. Mr. Addison pushed right back. But the others climbed over the rail, grabbed the rope and began to follow Mrs. Addison down towards the dock.

"Here you go, Henry," said his father as he lifted Henry over the rail.

"I can't, Dad!" shouted Henry.

"Yes you can!"

"No, I can't! Look!" Henry pointed at the rope. It had caught fire.

"Hurry!" they both shouted at Mrs. Addison.

She made it to the dock just in time. The others did not. The rope burned through, dropping them in the water into the treacherous space between the dock and the boat. Henry didn't see them come up.

"Get as far away as you can!" shouted Mr. Addison to his wife. "We'll find you!" Henry's dad grabbed his hand and made his way towards the flames. There had to be a way off somewhere.

Jack held out the emergency paddle from the *Shepherd* for the man to grab. It was hard work getting him in the boat, but desperation helped. After that, he had the man to help him with the others. For there were so many others. Jumping into the water was clearly the safest way off the *Noronic*, and bodies were falling from the inferno high above the *Shepherd* with horrific regularity.

Jack loaded as many as he thought the *Shepherd* could manage then putted over to the pier. Many hands reached down into the boat to help the survivors out. A policeman jumped in.

"You steer, kid. I'll rescue," he said gruffly. Jack guessed that it was a measure of the direness of the emergency that he wasn't sent home. The *Shepherd* went back into the harbour and Jack and the policeman peered into the dark water looking for bobbing heads. Two other policemen took off their coats and shoes and dove into the lake, helping those made unconscious by the terrible fall. One lady landed right on top of the water taxi, crashing through the cabin roof, spraying blood everywhere. But Ross Leitch's water taxi and the *Shepherd* kept going, back and forth, back and forth.

PULLING ON HENRY'S HAND, Mr. Addison made his way to the starboard side of "C" Deck. The *Kingston* was moored in the next slip, and her crew had man-handled a gangplank from the relatively safe deck of the *Kingston* to the burning *Noronic*. Passengers were crawling across it on hands and knees. Mr. Addison pushed Henry towards it. But once again they were too late.

The paint on the *Kingston* began to bubble from the heat of the fire. Flying embers had already started small fires on the *Cayuga*, on the other side, and she had been forced to steam away from the pier. To save the *Kingston,* she had to go too. As her engines came to life, the crew kept the gangplank in place for as long as they could, right until it crashed into the water as the *Kingston* fled to safety.

The water was their only hope. Mr. Addison made his way back towards the stern, taking the starboard side away from the fire. There was more open water there.

"See the little boats, Henry? When you come up, swim for the boats. I'll be right behind you."

Just then there was a shout from the water.

"Henry! Henry! It's me, Jack. Hurry up and jump. I'll pick you up! You gotta hurry!"

Mr. Addison lifted Henry over the railing. "I love you, Son," he said, and then he threw him overboard.

CHAPTER 32
One Short Hour

THE WATER WAS FREEZING COLD. THE FALL had taken hours, it seemed to Henry. When he crashed into the water, he was sure he was dead. Everything hurt. As he sank down through the black waters of the lake, Henry reckoned he must not be dead after all, to hurt so much. He struggled up to the surface.

Strong arms pulled him out of the water and dragged him face-first into a boat. Coughing and spluttering, he looked up and right into Jack's face.

"You okay?" asked Jack. His face was black with soot.

"Yeah," replied Henry. Then he sat straight up. "My dad! Where's my dad?

"DAD!" he shouted into the night.

"We're looking," said Jack. "Keep your eyes peeled. We didn't see anybody come over the rail after you, so maybe he hasn't jumped yet."

Henry kept his eyes glued to the *Noronic* until he had to look away from the bright glare. Where was his dad?

The *Shepherd* picked up a few more people then returned to deposit them on the pier.

"You can't leave without him!" cried Henry.

"We'll come back, son, if we need to," replied the policeman gently. "Maybe the water taxi picked him up."

Back at the pier, the survivors, including Henry, were lifted to shore. Ross Leitch followed them in. He spoke quietly to the policeman.

"No need for more trips," he said. "There's nobody left alive on that boat, that's for sure."

Jack looked back. It was true. Every inch of the *Noronic* was in flames. Nobody could survive that. The Queen was dead.

"Listen kid, go ahead and tie up," said the policeman. "I'll make one last pass in the water taxi. Why don't you stick with your friend? Help him find his family."

Jack motored away from the inferno and tied up. By now, there were lots of harbour police keeping the smaller boats at a safe distance. Jack climbed onto the pier and found Henry, who had been given a blanket but was still shivering.

"See your mom or dad yet?" he asked. "What do they look like?"

The two boys turned to scan the pier. It was pandemonium. One short hour earlier couples had been strolling along enjoying the warm breezes. The lights of the three cruise ships had been twinkling all in a row. The night watchman for Pier Nine had been making a routine inspection of the docks. Now the *Noronic* was completely ablaze and the other two ships were standing off, dark shadows in the lake, surrounded by small craft filled with reporters and photographers. Fire engines, police cars and ambulances were lined up along the avenue. Hundreds of people crowded onto the pier. Some were survivors. Some were not. Some were trying to help the dying. Others were there simply to gawk.

Jack thought that if he only had to take in the scene with his eyes, he could bear it. Horrible as it was, he felt he could cope if he could focus on the people who were finding their loved ones, on the doctors who had come to help and on the firefighters who were bravely fighting what all could see was a lost cause. But he couldn't just see.

Jack had to hear and smell.

Hear the piteous cries of the dying, calling out for help. Hear the keening of those who had lost friends or family. Hear the frantic shouts of emergency workers and the yowling sirens of their vehicles.

Smell the burnt flesh.

Above it all was the incessant wailing of the *Noronic*'s broken whistle. The Queen was dying, but she could not stop crying. The moaning went on and on.

CHAPTER 33
Help Arrives

Jack wondered how you knew if a person was in shock. He was worried about Henry. In spite of the blanket, Henry was still shaking, and he hardly seemed aware of what was going on. Jack was happy to help him find his parents, but he didn't know what they looked like. He needed Henry back.

Jack put his arm around Henry. "Hey, buddy, snap out of it!" Jack shook him a little. "We've got to find your dad, remember? What's he wearing?"

Henry didn't reply. He just stopped and stood staring at an elderly man in his underwear sitting on the concrete, with a white-haired lady cradled in his arms. The man was crying.

"Henry, Henry! Come on, let's go," Jack steered him away. "What colour hair has your mom got?"

"We're getting a new car, Jack," said Henry in a dreamy voice. "Did I tell you? A brand new Ford Dream Wagon. We're going to Washington to see the Lincoln Memorial. My dad's taking us."

"That's great, Henry," replied Jack, moving him away from a body covered in a sheet. "Let's look for your dad so you don't miss the trip." A policeman was handcuffing a man to a fence to stop him from going back on board to look for his family. The man was fighting like a tiger. Jack was getting scared. He didn't know what to do.

All of a sudden there was a frenzy of shouting. "Look out, look out!" The *Noronic* had begun to list dangerously away from Pier Nine. All the water that had been poured into her had obviously filled the cargo holds, shifting the centre of gravity. Everyone on shore held their breath to see if she would capsize. But with a great groan, the *Noronic* partially righted herself. Then there was a loud gurgling, sucking noise, and with a sigh the *Noronic* sank to the bottom. Only "A," "B" and "C" decks remained above the waterline. But they were still ablaze. The firemen went back to work, training their hoses on her once again.

"Henry! Henry!" It was Mrs. Addison, running across the pier towards them. "Oh, Henry," she cried, grabbing him into a tight hug, "I thought I'd lost you! Where's your dad?"

"Dead. Dad's dead," Henry said, still in that strange voice. "Mom, I don't like this boat trip. Let's get the car and go to Washington instead."

"Henry, what are you saying?" asked Mrs. Addison with fear in her eyes. "Henry, what's wrong with you?"

"Ma'am, he jumped into the water and got a little mixed up. I think he's okay, though. My name's Jack. I'm the one who took Henry sailing this evening, you know? I don't think your husband is dead. We just haven't found him yet."

"What on earth are you talking about?" Mrs. Addison looked at Jack as if he was a crazy person. "Henry has never been sailing. Who *are* you?"

"I'm Jack," he repeated patiently. This was the weirdest night he had ever had. "What's your husband's name? I'll go check with the police for you."

Leaving Henry with his mother, Jack escaped. He decided that he would concentrate on finding Henry's dad and that was all. Then he wouldn't have to think about all the other people. Or the *Noronic*. Or his dream. He headed over to a table manned by two people wearing Red Cross vests.

Jack wrote Mr. Addison's name on a list as "missing." "Are your friends hurt? Do they need a doctor?" asked the rescue workers.

"No, I don't think so," replied Jack.

"Okay. Kid, do you live here?"

Jack nodded his head. "Okay, take them to the Royal York Hotel, you know where that is?" Jack nodded again. "The whole city's turned out to help. The Royal York and the King Edward Hotel have opened their doors to anybody who needs a bed or something to eat. Doctors and nurses are coming in to help with the wounded. Maybe you should get your friends checked out at the hotel, just to be sure. If they need clothes or shoes, get them at the hotel. Donations are pouring in from all over the city." Jack nodded his thanks and started to walk away.

The rescue worker called after him. "And kid, if you don't think your friends can walk, take them to a taxi. We're all out of ambulances. But all the city taxi companies have joined together and are linked with emergency dispatch. They're available to take the wounded wherever they need to go. No charge. Got it?"

Jack nodded in amazement. How did all that happen so fast?

CHAPTER 34
One Friend
Very Early Saturday Morning

MRS. ADDISON AND HENRY HAD AGREED to follow Jack to the Royal York Hotel, for they didn't know what else to do. The hotel was an organized madhouse.

Earlier in the summer, a friend of Jack's mother had invited her to tea at the Royal York. Jack had come across on the ferry with her; he wanted a new Monopoly game and they were on sale at Eaton's for five dollars. Jack picked up the game, then met his mom at the Royal York for the return trip. He had never seen such an elegant place. Not that crystal chandeliers, fancy rugs and leather chesterfields were of great interest to him. But it looked swell, even Jack could tell.

At four o'clock in the morning in the middle of a disaster, the lobby was unrecognizable. Every leather chesterfield had become a fancy stretcher. Burns were being treated, intravenous drips started, wounds stitched. Doctors and nurses in street clothes moved from one patient to the next. Liveried hotel staff passed paper cups of hot coffee and tiny sandwiches on silver trays. Small knots of *Noronic* survivors, most dressed in nothing but nightclothes and greasy soot, clustered together exchanging stories. The Red Cross had set up shop on one of the mahogany dining tables, compiling still more lists of the missing, hurt and dead.

Jack checked his charges in at the Red Cross table. Then he found them some chairs in a corner. He brought them each a cup of hot coffee.

"My father drinks coffee," said Henry conversationally. "Where is he?"

Mrs. Addison looked at Jack expectantly, as if he should know. Jack looked around wildly. "The firemen are looking for him," he said. "They'll bring him here when they find him." Jack hoped that was true.

There was nothing more he could do for Henry. After promising to return the next day, Jack left the hotel and headed back to the *Shepherd*, taking a convoluted route that he hoped would avoid most of the congestion. And the sights. And smells.

Jack putted slowly across the bay in the *Shepherd*. Photographers with special nighttime cameras were being motored about the harbour. Jack waved to the Van Camps. They had a 14-footer with an 18 horsepower

Johnson outboard, so it was no surprise that they had been commandeered into service by the press.

By the time Jack made it back to Clapp's Cove, the sun was coming up and he was exhausted. And not at all ready to face the reception committee that awaited him. Standing there in the early dawn were most of the Ward's Islanders and they looked grim. Some of the dads helped pull the *Shepherd* up on shore and Jack was grateful for that small mercy. He was so tired. He closed his eyes and waited for the yelling to start.

"Jack, what were you thinking?" shrieked his mother. "You could have been killed out there!"

"You took the boat without permission. There was no way we could go after you and bring you back. Or send some real help to the *Noronic*!" That came from Beans's dad.

"You always have to be the hero, don't you? What about your poor mother, left here wringing her hands after you?" Jack wasn't sure who that was.

"This stunt was downright reckless!" That was definitely Dougie and Donnie's father.

Lucy Mae sidled up to Jack and pretended to help him tie up the *Shepherd*. "Did you get Henry out?" she whispered urgently.

"Yeah, I fished him out of the lake. But we couldn't find his dad," Jack said quietly.

Jack hardly heard the next few comments. But he couldn't tune out the last one.

"I'm so disappointed in you, Jack," said his father quietly. Jack sagged.

"ENOUGH!"

All the islanders stopped short and looked up. Captain Clapp had been standing in the shadows. Nobody had seen him.

"Can't you see the boy's exhausted? Is this really the time to tell him how foolhardy he is, how inconsiderate, how thoughtless? Because he is, we all know that. But he's also a Ward's Islander, and tonight he proved that in spades! Was William Ward being smart, or cautious, when he chipped ten frozen men from the rigging of the *Jane Ann*? There was a maritime emergency in our harbour tonight, and for all that young Jack is — or isn't — he's a mariner in his heart and soul. I don't think he could have stopped himself from going in, however foolish it may have been.

"And," the Captain went on, fixing Jack with a ferocious look, "it *was* foolish. Don't you forget it, boy."

There was silence in the Cove.

"How many did you pull from the water tonight, Jack?" asked the Captain gravely.

"Between the *Shepherd* and the water taxi, maybe fifty," stammered Jack.

"Fifty people," repeated the Captain. "And the way I hear it," he went on, looking at Lucy Mae, "one of them was a friend."

"Yes," said Jack in a stronger voice. "Fifty. And one a friend."

CHAPTER 35
Mother and Son
Saturday

J ACK SLEPT UNTIL NOON. WHEN HE FINALLY made his way out to the kitchen, he found his mom serving pancakes to the whole crew.

"About time, sleepyhead," said Dougie. "We thought you were never going to wake up!"

Jack plunked himself down on a chair. "I hurt all over," he groaned.

"Not surprising, young man," retorted his mother primly, as she turned to pour more batter onto the griddle.

Jack leaned over to Donnie. "Is she still mad?" he whispered.

"Nobody's mad," Donnie whispered back.

"After you left the Cove, the Captain yelled at everybody. Told them you'd done the right thing, that you were thinking like a man," added Dougie.

"'Speed was of the essence' – that's what he said," Beans went on. "You're off the hook – no punishment, lucky devil." Beans sighed dramatically. "You *always* get away with everything."

Mrs. Gordon came back to the table with a steaming platter of pancakes, cutting the whispered conversation short. "You're lucky that you weren't badly hurt or killed, Jack," said his mother. "I know this is all very exciting, but the wreck is off limits to you from this point forward. I'm serious Jack, that's final. You may *not* go back there today."

Jack sucked in his breath. "Mom, after what I saw last night, I don't want to go back."

"Good," she said.

"But I have to."

"Jack! Enough! You are not going anywhere!" his mother shouted. Interested, the crew leaned forward, turning their eyes back to Jack. He usually won arguments with his mother, but this would be a toughie.

"Mom, remember I told you last night that I rescued Henry? He's from Detroit. We went over to the *Noronic* yesterday and he invited us all aboard. To thank him, we took him sailing. Right, guys?" There were nods all around the table.

"Last night his mom got off the *Noronic,* then Henry's dad threw him overboard from one of the top decks. His dad was supposed to jump afterwards, but he didn't. I pulled Henry out of the water, but we couldn't find his dad."

Mrs. Gordon looked aghast, putting her hand to her throat. "He threw his son *overboard*?"

"There was no other way, Mom. After that I took Henry and his mom to the Royal York Hotel like the policeman told me to. I promised I'd come back today to help them look for Henry's dad. I promised, Mom. They don't know anybody but us."

Mrs. Gordon sat down heavily in the last free chair. "How do you get into such situations, Jack?" She shook her head wryly. "A promise is a promise. You knew I'd have no choice but to say that, didn't you?" Jack grinned.

"All right, but there are conditions. You will take the ferry, not the prams. You will go straight to the Royal York Hotel. I daresay that by the time you get there the authorities will already have helped your friend and you won't be needed anyway. You will NOT hang about the pier, gawking. You will NOT get in the way of the emergency workers. And you WILL be back here by dark. Do you hear, young man?"

Wolfing down the last of his pancakes, Jack nodded vigorously. "Thanks, Mom." Then to his friends, Jack added, "Meet you at the ferry docks."

In moments the kids had dumped their breakfast dishes in the sink, said a quick thank you to Mrs. Gordon, and slammed the screen door behind them.

Jack pulled on his clothes and made for the door to follow them. Then he stopped, and looked back at his mother. He crossed the floor in two steps and gave her a big hug.

"I'm scared, Mom. What if we can't find Henry's dad?"

Mrs. Gordon held her son tightly. "I don't know, Jack. It's a terrible thing. If it were me, I don't know if I could bear it." She held Jack at arm's length and looked into his worried face. "I'll pray that you find him."

CHAPTER 36
A New Toothbrush

THE CREW WAS GLUED TO THE STARBOARD side of the *Sam McBride* as the ferry made its ten-minute run to the city. The *Noronic* was still smouldering. Charred life jackets, deck chairs and pieces of wood filled the harbour. The kids could see rescue workers moving up and down two temporary gangplanks placed across from the dock to "C" deck, carrying out stretchers. All the stretchers were covered in sheets. Lucy Mae had to cover her eyes.

"Wow," breathed Beans.

Once on the other side, the crew made their way up the hill to the Royal York Hotel, just two blocks away. At first a policeman refused them entry, but Jack's honeyed tongue managed to sweet-talk the whole crew inside. They found Henry and his mother still sitting in the chairs Jack had left them in. Both had changed from their dirty, wet nightclothes to brand new trousers and shirts. Mrs. Addison had forgotten to remove the price tag from hers. They both looked awfully pale.

"Henry?" asked Jack cautiously. "Remember us?"

"Jack! You came back!"

Jack heaved a sigh of relief. Henry was back from that strange place he had been the night before. "I promised I'd come. Have you found your dad yet?"

Henry shook his head sadly. "The Red Cross people have been calling all the hospitals for us. Nobody's seen him. But," he added a bit more hopefully, "there are a lot of people in hospital who just can't talk, so they can't tell anybody who they are. Their throats are burned, you see? That's probably where Dad is."

"I'm sure you're right," said Jack. "That's why we came to help. Maybe we can go to the hospitals and check them out. Do you have a picture of your dad?"

"We haven't got anything," said Mrs. Addison. "Nothing but what has been given to us by strangers." She looked down at her new clothes. From her pocket she pulled out a new toothbrush. "A man came this morning. He said he owned a drugstore. He brought boxes of toothbrushes. It's all we've got."

Lucy Mae went up to Mrs. Addison and gave her a little hug. "You've got Henry and you've got us," she said gently.

"But who *are* you all?" asked Mrs. Addison in confusion.

Just then a Red Cross worker came over. "Mrs. Addison, I'm very sorry, but we are asking those who have a loved one missing to come with us. Bodies taken from the *Noronic* have been taken to the Horticulture Building at the Canadian National Exhibition. We need family members to make identifications. Your husband is probably not there, but we are asking if you will come with us just to rule it out."

The group looked at the emergency worker in horror. Identify a body? She had to be kidding. But she wasn't. Mrs. Addison didn't even know Lucy Mae's name, but in desperation she clutched her and began to weep. Lucy Mae patted her back, not knowing what else to do.

"We'll go with you," she said bravely.

"I'm sorry," said the Red Cross lady, "but we are only transporting immediate family members. You will have to wait here."

Henry looked at Jack in panic. "Don't worry," said Jack quietly. "We'll take the streetcar and probably get there before you. Look for us at the Princes' Gate."

"Where?" cried Henry, but the crew was already gone, out the hotel door, racing for the streetcar stop.

CHAPTER 37
The Horticulture Building
Canadian National Exhibition

B Y THE TIME THE CREW GOT TO THE CNE, there was a lineup at the gate. Police were checking people through, making sure that only family members got inside. And they were only allowing adults.

"But he's my son!" cried Mrs. Addison. "I want him with me!"

Jack stepped up to the plate, but even he couldn't convince the policeman to let Henry through. Jack pulled Mrs. Addison out of line.

"Don't you worry," he said. "These are the Toronto Fairgrounds. When the Exhibition is going on we, ah, well, we sort of know how to sneak in." Jack felt uncomfortable admitting this to a grown-up.

"Anyway, we know how to get to the Horticulture Building without the police seeing. We'll take Henry and meet you there."

Mrs. Addison looked confused, but she agreed to let Henry go with them. The crew took Henry to their special spot, a small hole in the fence near the Flyer roller coaster. Mrs. Addison was waiting for them at the Horticulture Building.

Security was unhappy but assumed the police had allowed Henry in, so they let him into the building. The crew watched as Henry and his mother went inside. It was a terrible place. Many people came out crying. Some were so upset they had to be helped by doctors or nurses. Jack prayed Mr. Addison wasn't inside.

The crew waited a long time for Henry and his mom to come out. When they did, Mrs. Addison was distraught. Henry's face was puffy from crying. Nobody needed to ask what they had found out.

Mr. Addison was inside. At least, his gold watch was. He hadn't managed to make it off the *Noronic* in time.

THE CREW WALKED SILENTLY back to the Princes' Gate to get Mrs. Addison into the taxi queue. As they waited, Henry turned to Jack.

"What do I do, Jack? I don't know what I'm supposed to do!"

A taxi rolled up. Jack thought fast. "Get your mom back to the hotel. We'll meet you there. Don't worry about anything, okay?"

Henry nodded. As the taxi drove away, Jack hurried the crew to the streetcar stop. "Here's the plan. We need to take them home with us. We need to make them safe. Mrs. Addison seems to like Lucy, so she and I will go back to the Royal York. The rest of you, stay on the streetcar and go straight down to the docks. Lucy and I will get Henry and his mom ready to go, then we'll follow you. That'll take a while; they might not want to go back, so we'll have to take a route that doesn't take us close to Pier Nine. You'll get back to the island way before us."

The crew nodded. "Okay, Jack. Then what?"

Jack thought for a moment.

"Get the moms."

CHAPTER 38
The Addisons Come Home

ENRY AND MRS. ADDISON WERE BARELY aware of their surroundings, they were so tied up in their knot of grief. Jack and Lucy Mae had an easy time convincing them to come home with the islanders. Lucy Mae talked to the Red Cross people, explaining where the Addisons were going, while Jack prowled outside the hotel, looking for a willing driver.

Lots of people had come to help the survivors, so it wasn't hard to find somebody with a car. Jack explained that he wanted to stay away from Pier Nine and the driver nodded his head.

"No problem, kid. I couldn't get you close to the *Noronic* even if I wanted to. They've got the whole place sealed off."

That was a relief. Jack went back inside and helped Henry with his mother. Lucy Mae sat beside Mrs. Addison in the back seat and held her hand. On the ferry, they took care to sit on the side that faced away from Pier Nine. To Jack, it was the longest ferry ride he'd ever taken. It should have been pretty — he was facing west and the sun was setting, making the water glitter with rubies. The breeze was lovely, blowing away the smell of the fire. But for the first time, Jack couldn't enjoy the wind and the waves. He didn't want to pretend to be captain of the ferry.

Boats weren't safe.

It wasn't a direct ferry. The *Sam McBride* crossed first to Hanlan's Point, then made its way to Centre Island. Loads of Saturday picnickers piled on to return to the city. They were laughing. How could they laugh? It was nearly dark by the time the ferry docked at Ward's Island.

Lucy Mae took Mrs. Addison's arm to help her onto the dock. Henry took her other arm. Jack followed behind. Waiting for them were the island moms.

They were all there. Mrs. Gordon had an afghan. She wrapped it around Mrs. Addison's shoulders, then took over from Lucy Mae. "We're taking you to Missy Clapp. She's got a quiet place for you and your boy." Nothing else was said.

The moms formed a protective circle around Mrs. Addison as they led her to Channel Avenue. Jack hadn't noticed at first, but the dads were standing quietly nearby with the rest of the crew. They silently fell into place behind the women. Dougie and Donnie's dad nodded in Jack's direction.

He'd done the right thing bringing the Addisons home. For once in his life, he'd made a good plan. Jack stepped into line with the men, following the group to Channel Avenue.

The Captain was waiting on his porch. He took Mrs. Addison's hand, holding it briefly in sympathy. Then he stepped away to let the women inside.

Missy Clapp wasn't sitting in her regular chair, but was ensconced on the chesterfield. She lifted her arms to Mrs. Addison.

"Come here, my dear," she said kindly. "Sit beside me." Mrs. Addison, looking somewhat dazed by the attention, sat down. "We are so very sorry," Missy Clapp said. She put her arms around Mrs. Addison. Tears began to stream down Mrs. Addison's cheeks. Without thinking, she rested her head on this stranger's ample bosom and wept.

CHAPTER 39
The Addisons Go Home
Sunday

JACK WAS AWAKENED THE NEXT MORNING BY the foghorn. He was an island boy, and usually the gloomy sound didn't register, he'd heard it so often. But this morning it matched his mood. Grey clouds swirled over the harbour, obscuring the city and blotting out Pier Nine. Jack tried to pretend that the Queen wasn't resting on the bottom of the lake, that Henry's father was still alive. But he couldn't.

The island moms and dads had taken over the care of the Addisons. The Captain had telephoned Henry's aunt and uncle in Cleveland. They were driving to Toronto to fetch them home. Until then, the Addisons would stay in the little cottage on Channel Avenue. Everyone on Ward's went about their business quietly, respecting the family's grief. Henry and his mom stayed inside with Missy Clapp.

All that grey day and the next, Jack and the crew lounged about in the Wiman Shelter. For the first time that summer, they didn't know what to do with themselves. Finally they got out their ukuleles. Strumming listlessly, they jumped from song to song, finishing none of them. Nobody sang. Then there was a knock at the door.

It was the Captain. "The Addisons are leaving," he said. "We thought you kids might want to say goodbye."

The crew trooped down to the ferry dock. Mrs. Addison and Henry were standing with two strangers, their relatives probably, and a few of the moms and dads. Everyone was shaking hands gravely. Jack stuck his hand out to Henry. "Maybe you can come back one summer and stay with us," he said.

"Will you teach me to sail?" asked Henry.

"If you want," replied Jack.

"My mom might not want to," sighed Henry, "but I'll ask. I'd like that." Henry raised his eyes to Jack's. "Thanks."

"Yeah," said Jack. And that was goodbye.

CHAPTER 40
Decisions
Wednesday

THE SABOT PRAMS OF THE COVE FLEET RESTED quietly on their racks all week. Nobody wanted to go sailing and have to dodge the grisly debris still cluttering the harbour. Nobody wanted to see the blackened, twisted corpse of the Queen of the Inland Seas. But the Cup was coming. Sailors from Oakville, Montreal and Rochester would be arriving for the international regatta, expecting to meet the Cove Fleet on the course. Captain Clapp and the race committee called a meeting with the boys so they could decide what to do. Jack got to the Clubhouse early.

"Captain Clapp, I've got to ask you something," Jack said urgently. "Was the *Noronic* cursed?"

Captain Clapp looked thoughtful. Then he said, "I don't know, Jack. I just don't know. I've heard the story. Seafaring people are a superstitious lot. Who knows if it means anything?"

"I've been thinking. I mean, I can't stop thinking. Where was the captain?" Jack clenched his fists. "How could he let all those people die?"

The Captain lit his pipe.

"Tell you the truth, Jack, I've been thinking about it too. The papers say he was there. They say he was one of the last off and the firemen had to drag him away. He was just standing there on the deck, his boots melting, holding a firehose that had no water coming out."

The Captain sighed. "Jack, it may be that once that fire started, there was no way anybody could stop it. Not even the captain. It could be that the captain wasn't well prepared. It hurts my heart to think that, but maybe it's true. Nobody knows, except the captain himself. And prepared or not, he has to live with what happened. Well over a hundred dead, all while tied up to the dock. It's hard to imagine."

The Captain sat down heavily on a bench. "Jack, you said once that a captain was like a king. And that's a great thing to be when you're standing way up there on the bridge and the wind is blowing your way. But a tragedy like this, it's also a captain's lot. Do you still want it?"

"Hey there, are you starting without us?" The rest of the island sailors were arriving. The dads who were on the race committee were coming in too. Captain Clapp looked hard at Jack. "You think about it, boy. You think real hard."

The Captain called the meeting to order and got right to the point. "Do you boys want to cancel the regatta?" he asked bluntly.

The boys looked at one another. Then they looked at Jack. "I can't speak for the crew," said Jack, shrugging his shoulders. "I don't have a boat, so I don't have a vote."

Mr. Gordon spoke up. "The race committee has discussed your situation, Jack. It is the general feeling among us –" at this, Jack's dad glanced at the Captain – "that you have earned *Frosty Friday* back."

The crew erupted in hoots and hollers. Jack smiled, but sat quietly. He'd gained one boat by losing another. It was hard to feel happy. The loss, his and Henry's and everybody else's, was too fresh.

But the decision still had to be made. The crew waited for Jack to weigh in. Jack sighed. "If it was up to me, I'd say I don't want to go back into the harbour. I don't want to be reminded."

Captain Clapp had taken his pipe out of his mouth and was looking hard at Jack, waiting to see what more he'd say. Jack swallowed.

"But we have to go. We've all heard the Captain's stories. There have been boats on the lakes forever. And more disasters than we can count. We've got to keep sailing." Jack stood up, flashing a shadow of his old grin. "And we've got to be the best!"

All the sailors leapt to their feet and cheered. Jack looked over at the Captain. He was smiling.

It was decided after consulting with the weatherman and the Commodores of the other sailing clubs that the regatta would be moved out of the harbour and into the lake. It was heavier water out there, with more swells and waves than in the sheltered harbour, but the weather report said the day would be fine and the prams, though tiny, were very reliable. The decision was made. The Cup would go on.

CHAPTER 41
The Cup
Saturday

RACE DAY DAWNED FINE AND SUNNY. THE crew was down at Clapp's Cove bright and early to prepare their boats. For Jack, it was like coming home. *Frosty Friday* was a part of him, and it had felt a little like he was missing an arm or a leg when she had been beached without him. As Jack rinsed her down and raised the sail, he murmured to her under his breath. He told her about the horrors he had seen. Jack had already told the crew about that night, playing up all the excitement, but there was a lot he'd left out.

The bad bits, the bits that kept him awake at night, the bits that made him afraid. He hadn't told his father or Captain Clapp either. Besides *Frosty Friday*, only his mother knew everything. She was the one who held him when he cried. His mother knew every detail.

And Jack had told Lucy Mae some of it too, but he wasn't sure why. She'd asked the right questions, he guessed, and he couldn't help himself. And somehow he knew that she would never tell anybody. It actually made him feel better knowing that she knew. Weird.

Because the visiting sailors couldn't drive their boat trailers on the island, they all had to leave them on the mainland and sail over. Around about eleven in the morning, the crew could see a mass of colourful sails crossing the harbour. When the visitors arrived in the Cove, they were full of questions about the *Noronic*.

"Did you see the fire? What was it like? Any dead bodies float over? How close did you get?" The questions kept coming and coming. Finally the moms arrived with sandwiches and lemonade for lunch, and Jack had some peace and quiet while they filled their faces.

After lunch the markers were loaded into the *Shepherd* and the race committee putted away. Captain Clapp gathered all the sailors together to give them their instructions.

"You'll head out through the Eastern Gap into the lake proper to avoid the debris. The Gap will be a tight squeeze, since there are so many of you, so try not to swamp each other before the race even starts!" Everybody laughed.

"You are all accomplished sailors and we have no concerns about you sailing in the lake. As you can see, it's a fine, calm day. But I want to remind you that the weather can change at any moment. We're at the end of the season and squalls can come across the lake without warning. Watch for them, just in case. If the race committee feels that the weather is deteriorating, we'll signal you with the red and white 'return to shore' flag. Does everyone understand? All the sailors nodded.

"We'll also be flying the red and yellow flag. Does everyone know what that means?" There were groans all around. "Right. Life jackets at all times. No exceptions!"

Anticipation was pushing thoughts of the *Noronic* out of Jack's brain. It felt good to focus on the race. As he made his final adjustments, he sensed Lucy Mae standing behind him.

"Good luck, Jack. I hope you win."

"Thanks. Me too."

"How do the pieces look today?" she asked seriously.

Just as seriously, Jack looked around at the other sailors who were all wearing their team jerseys. "It's going to be a tough race. See that guy in the blue hat? He's a really good sailor, especially in heavy weather, because he's so strong. I bet he's eighteen. But he's a dirty racer: he cheats. He's got to be watched. And that girl from Rochester in the striped shorts? She comes every year. She's known for staying behind on the first two legs, then taking the lead at the end. She drives me crazy." Jack looked at Lucy.

"I guess the pieces are okay. I know most of these racers, so I can guess what they'll do. But I'll have to watch out for surprises. I think there's going to be a big one today," he added.

"What kind of a surprise?" asked Lucy Mae.

"We're going to get weather," Jack replied, as he pushed *Frosty Friday* off the beach. "I'm sure of it."

Lucy Mae looked up at the sky. It was a beautiful day without a single cloud in the sky. Maybe Jack wasn't as smart as she'd thought.

CHAPTER 42
The Flag

ELPING HANDS PUSHED THE PRAMS OFF THE beach and the boats headed to the Gap. Lucy Mae tried to talk her way onto the *Shepherd,* but with no luck. So once the crew was off, she raced to the breakwater of the Gap to watch them sail by. Here at least, the prams were close enough to see. When the race started they would be too far away, and the very exciting afternoon would become abysmally boring. Boy, she wished she had a boat too.

It was quite a parade. More than fifty sabot prams passed through the Gap, using the same waterway that had brought the *Noronic* to Toronto a short week earlier. Jack tried not to think about it. Dougie was busy waving to the crowd on shore, clowning around like he always did. They reached the start line out in the lake at the same time, and grinned as they took their nervous pee together. The starter's pistol went, and they were off.

The first race was a disaster. The wind was all over the place and Jack had to fight for every scrap of forward motion. Rounding the last marker, Jack took a chance. Blue Hat was right behind him, so Jack cut the turn as close as he could. Too close. He touched the mark. Hollers of glee erupted from the boat just behind him. Blue Cap was overjoyed that the sea lawyers would disqualify Jack.

The second race was a squeaker. The wind changed direction just before the finish, leaving Jack dead in the water. The girl in the striped shorts kept as close as she could to the wind, what little there was, and inched her way past Jack toward the finish line. It was painful to watch. Jack knew there had to be some wind somewhere. At the last minute, only a hundred yards from the finish, Jack all of a sudden turned about and sailed parallel to the finish line. There was the wind. He picked up speed, then jibbed back. If he was lucky, the momentum would carry him over the line. It did. He lost his wind but was going fast enough to cruise over the line just ahead of the girl from Rochester. The race was his.

The whole crew was totally psyched for the third and final race. Jack was in his element. The wind was picking up, the sun was shining, his crew was beside him, the Captain was watching and he had a crack at the Cup. He just had to pull off the last race. All the pieces had fallen into just the right places.

The starter's pistol went for the last time that afternoon. Jack got a bad start, but no matter, there was time to recover. Donnie was really flying, way ahead of the pack. Jack squinted through the sun sparkles dancing on the water. Where had Donnie found that wind?

Jack tacked and followed Donnie. There it was! A wonderful gust coming across the lake filled their sails. They were one-two around the first marker. Side by side, they found a great header on the second leg and pulled well ahead of the pack. At one point, they started whooping as loudly as they could just for the sheer joy of being on the water. The last marker was still a ways ahead and both boys were paying more attention to having fun than to the race. Why not? Unless disaster struck, they were so far ahead they couldn't lose.

The squall came from the south, from behind them. All at once the wind died and there was an unearthly silence. Most people wouldn't have noticed the change but Jack could feel it in his bones. Instinctively he lowered his sail. He yelled to Donnie who was still ahead but all sound seemed to be dampened. Donnie didn't hear.

Jack looked behind him. A grey wall of rain was approaching from across the lake. It hit the rest of the boats first and Jack saw pram after pram go over, dumping their sailors into the lake. Urgently Jack shouted to Donnie, "Get your sail down!" But Donnie still couldn't hear.

Jack hunkered down as the wall passed over him. *Frosty Friday* bobbed around like a cork but didn't turn turtle. Ahead, Donnie was fiddling with his sail, trying to find the wind that had disappeared. He never saw the gust coming. The squall caught his sail with such force that it broke the boom and wind spilled out of the flapping sail. The release of all that tension shot the broken boom out like an arrow. It hit Donnie on the side of his head and launched him overboard. The pram followed, turning on its side where the sail kept it from going all the way over. Donnie was caught somewhere underneath all that canvas.

Jack grabbed his paddle and frantically fought the churning water. It felt like hours, not minutes, had passed by the time he got to Donnie. Jack used the paddle to lift sections of the sopping sail out of the water until he spotted the bright orange of Donnie's life jacket. Hooking the strap, he dragged Donnie by the collar towards *Frosty Friday*, then floated him around to the back of the pram. Reaching over with both arms, Jack hauled Donnie up and over the transom.

For a second, Donnie's face turned into Henry's. Jack shook his head to clear his vision and kept pulling until an unconscious Donnie flopped into the pram. Blooded welled out of his cut forehead.

What had Mr. Livingston taught them in Supervision? You had to do something with the person's neck, and then breathe into their mouth or something. Or were you supposed to pump the water out of their chest first? Jack couldn't remember. Where was the *Shepherd*? He needed help, fast.

Jack scanned the lake behind him. The red and white "return to shore" flag was up. The *Shepherd* was busy motoring around the bulk of the fleet, hauling sorry-looking sailors out of the drink and ferrying them to the Ward's Island beach. Captainless prams were floating all over the place. The *Shepherd* was going to be busy for a while. Jack couldn't tell if anybody even noticed that he and Donnie were so far out to the west. They were all alone.

CHAPTER 43
Drifting

ROSTY *FRIDAY* WAS DRIFTING INTO SHORE, just like all the other prams behind her. It was the way the lake worked on that side of the island. Trouble was, she was drifting towards Gibraltar Point, much further west than Jack wanted to go. "Goldarnit!" shouted Jack in frustration. "Goldarnit, goldarnit!!" He wanted to get to shore. Donnie seemed to be breathing, so he wasn't drowned, but he was still unconscious and bleeding. Jack's arms were getting tired from all the paddling. He sat back on his knees for a moment to take a break, and looked around.

Jack could still spot the *Shepherd* out in the water, but *Frosty Friday* had drifted so far west that he couldn't see the Ward's Island beach any more. Jack

hoped all the other sailors were all right. He looked at
the sky. The squall had passed through and the rain had
lightened to a mere shower. Looking east, Jack could
see the beginnings of blue sky. Typical squall, he
thought in disgust. It wrecks everything, then a half
hour later it's like it never happened. Jack sniffed the
wind. It was still a bit gusty. Did he dare? If he raised
the sail, he could get Donnie back to shore so much
sooner. And he might even be able to get the pram
closer to Ward's Island. But it was risky. If he caught a
gust with Donnie hurt, they'd be in real trouble.

Donnie groaned. "My head hurts!" Sitting up,
Donnie put his hand to his head and then stared at the
blood that came away on his fingers. "I'm bleeding!"
he said in surprise. "What happened?"

"Squall," said Jack shortly. Donnie nodded, then
winced. Donnie knew all about squalls.

"I didn't see it," he said. "I didn't see it coming."

"None of the boats did," replied Jack. "Almost
everybody went into the drink. The *Shepherd's* busy
hauling them out. Are you okay?"

"Yeah, I think," replied Donnie, moving gingerly.
"Where's my pram?"

Jack pointed behind them. "It'll drift in, don't
worry. There'll be a major salvage along the beach
after this race!"

Donnie tried to laugh with Jack but groaned
instead. "I feel sick."

Jack made a decision. "The wind's dying down. There might be another gust, but I don't think so. I'm going to raise the sail to get us in faster. Can you handle it?"

Donnie said he could, then kneeled low in the boat, looking for a position that would protect his aching head the most. Jack raised the sail and pulled on the sheet, looking for air that was going their way. But the wind was unpredictable.

"Where are you, you miserable piece of air, where are you?!" Jack shouted. And the wind came.

Frosty Friday flew. Donnie had never felt anything like it. He'd sailed against Jack a million times but not ever *with* him. Donnie had never felt a boat move like *Frosty Friday*. It was a revelation. Jack was not just a good sailor; he wasn't just taming the wind and the waves, he was a part of them. For the first time Donnie understood that Jack wasn't just his best bud, but something different, something special. His Captain.

Jack gained some ground to the east, but not enough. They missed Gibraltar Point but landed on the Centre Island beach. It was going to be a long walk along the Boardwalk for a guy who probably had a concussion. This wasn't over yet.

CHAPTER 44
Biking the Boardwalk

THE BEACH AT WARD'S WAS CROWDED WITH people. The spectators had rushed back to their cottages to collect blankets and towels for the bedraggled sailors. A huge bonfire roared. Missy Clapp was back at her cottage, and the Supervision girls were running back and forth between 2 Channel Avenue and the beach with hot pots of coffee and cocoa. Squall stories were being kicked about between some of the sailors and the onlookers. Other sailors were anxiously keeping their eyes on their prams, monitoring their progress as the boats drifted towards shore. The *Shepherd* had pulled all the people from the water and was now working at "herding" the drifting prams to soft beach landings.

Lucy Mae picked her way through all the people on the beach, balancing a tray of sandwiches. After depositing them on a picnic table, where they were eagerly snapped up by cold sailors, she went looking for her brother. He was listening to Blue Cap brag about his harrowing experience.

"Hey," she interrupted. "Where's the crew?"

Charles pointed towards the water's edge. "Down there, looking for their boats."

Lucy Mae squinted into the ever-brightening sunshine. "I see Beans and Dougie. Where's Jack? And Donnie? Didn't they come back?"

Charles frowned. "I'm pretty sure I saw them a minute ago," he replied. "But now that you ask, I'm not certain it was them."

"Hey, are you listening or what?" demanded Blue Cap.

"Yeah, great story, see ya," Charles said, vaguely waving as he left the group. "Haven't you seen them?"

"No. They couldn't… I mean, they couldn't still be in the lake, could they?" Lucy Mae asked anxiously.

"Naw. The *Shepherd* would've seen them, don't you think?" Charles bit his lip.

"We should look for them!" Tears were glistening in Lucy Mae's eyes.

"Hang on, don't you think their parents are looking?"

"Mr. Gordon is out in the *Shepherd*. And Mrs. Gordon is helping Missy Clapp with the food. They probably think Jack's already on shore. Nobody has been reported missing."

Charles sighed, then gazed down the beach. "Let's say they were ahead. That's likely, right?" That made Lucy Mae smile through her tears. "Where would they be?" Lucy Mae pointed to the west. "Over that way."

"Okay," said Charles slowly. "The boats are all drifting to shore. What's the next beach down?"

"Centre," said Lucy.

"Right. So we should get the bikes and…"

"Bike the Boardwalk! We'll find them! You're so smart, Charles!" Lucy Mae threw her arms around her brother then started running for home and her bike. Charles, somewhat bemused, ran after her.

DONNIE WAS HAVING A HARD TIME. His head really hurt and it was making him feel sick. And it just wouldn't stop bleeding. Jack had Donnie's arm around his shoulder and was trying to help him along. They looked like a couple of drunken sailors staggering along the Boardwalk. Jack tried to keep Donnie going by repeating some of the Captain's stories.

"So you're Rademuller, right. And I'm the soldier wanting some beer. And you'd better give it to me, or I'll throw you off the lighthouse!" Donnie smiled weakly.

Jack was just coming to the conclusion that he'd be better off leaving Donnie and running to Ward's to get help when he heard a shout. It was Charles.

"There they are! Come on, Lucy Mae!" Charles shouted. Jack was never so happy to see anybody in his life.

"Hey, what took you so long?!" Jack shouted.

"We've been pretty busy you know," Charles shot back, "rescuing all you guys. It was just a baby storm after all. Don't you guys know what you're doing out there?"

Jack laughed, and punched him lightly on the arm. "You're okay, Charlie. More than okay. You got character, just like your bike!" Charles went red.

They got Donnie perched on Charles's back fender, holding on tight. He got blood all over Charles's shirt, but nobody cared. Jack hopped up behind Lucy. By the time the foursome got back to Ward's beach, heads had been counted and the alert was out for the two missing sailors. As the two bikes came into view, a great cheer went up.

CHAPTER 45
"Windy Old Weather"

B LUE CAP WON THE CUP. WITH THE THIRD race scrapped, he and Jack had one race each but the sea lawyers decided that Blue Cap had more points.

It didn't seem to matter any more. There was a huge feast set up in the Clubhouse for the sailors and their families, and of course everybody on the island came too. Jack thought he was getting more attention because he lost the race than he used to get when he won, which didn't make sense. Donnie got a lot of attention too. He arrived late at the feast with a big bandage on his head and instructions from the doctor to "take it easy" for a few days. There was no end of little kids — and girls — who wanted to fetch and carry for him, and Donnie enjoyed every minute.

But the best part of the evening came just after the presentations. Jack had just shaken Blue Cap's hand when the Captain arrived. He took Jack aside and solemnly shook Jack's hand.

"You did well today, Jack," said the Captain. "You kept your head, thought things through and led your friend out of danger. I'd always hoped you had it in you to be a captain, and today you showed me I was right. I'm proud of you, Jack."

What a night.

When the food was cleared away, most of the visiting sailors had to make their way back to the mainland. Goodbyes were said and promises made to meet the next year in Rochester. Once they were gone, the entertainment committee set up for the Saturday dance. Most of the crew took the opportunity to hightail it to the Shelter, keeping themselves well away from the prospect of asking somebody up on the dance floor. Ugh.

But Jack stayed.

"Do you want to dance?" he asked Lucy Mae. "Just once, I mean, before we meet the guys?"

"Just once," smiled Lucy Mae.

After the dance, the two of them strolled back to Jack's house so he could get his uke to take to the Shelter.

"Do you think you'll come back next summer?" asked Jack.

"I want to. Even Charles wants to! We asked our parents but it depends on whether there's a cottage to rent. If there is, my dad says he'll get us each a pram."

"That'd be great," said Jack.

"Jack, do you think we'll ever see Henry again?"

"Doubt it. His mom won't want to come back here and have to pass Pier Nine every time she goes to the city."

"I wish Henry could come," said Lucy Mae sadly. "I think he needs us."

"Yeah, but there's nothing we can do." Jack shrugged his shoulders.

"Maybe there is," mused Lucy Mae. "You may be good at putting the pieces together on the water, Jack Gordon, but I'm pretty good on land. I'm going to write to him. Even if he can't come back, we can still stay friends. We'll just see."

Jack looked at Lucy Mae strangely. He couldn't imagine writing letters to anybody. "If you do, Lucy, tell him I'm his friend too."

The crew was mellow, strumming quietly in the Shelter. There was another kind of sadness that night. The last race was over; it was the end of the summer. In a week or so most of the island families would be closing their cottages up and moving back to their city homes. The island kids would return to their winter schools and their winter friends. Winter was never as good as summer.

"Let's pick up the pace, guys, or you're all going to be blubbering!" laughed Jack as he and Lucy Mae arrived at the Shelter. "Get the lead out!"

Everybody laughed with Jack and sat up a little straighter. The strumming picked up. Beans started "Andy the Handy Man" and before long everybody was singing "Bell Bottom George." They made Lucy Mae laugh with "Biceps, Muscle and Brawn." Then as the night grew late, they slowed it down a bit.

"Last song, guys," said Jack. "What'll it be?"

Donnie, his black hair flopping over the bandage on his head, strummed a chord or two. "Lucy, sing for us."

Lucy Mae thought for a minute. Then in a clear, sweet voice she began to sing "Windy Old Weather." The whole crew joined in on the chorus.

Come all you sailors, now listen to me
I'll sing you a song of the fish of the sea

In this windy old weather
Stormy old weather
When the wind blows
We'll all pull together.

Dear Henry,

I hope this letter finds you well. I got your address from Missy Clapp. She said you moved to Cleveland to stay with your aunt and uncle for a while. How is that? I bet you miss your friends in Detroit, but probably your mother is happy to be with her sister. How is she feeling?

There was one last sailing race after you left. We had a big storm. Donnie's boom broke and Jack lost the race.

Most of the crew has left Ward's Island for the winter. I don't like being at home because I miss everybody. I miss you too. So does Jack. He said to tell you that he's your friend. So am I.

Sincerely,
Lucy Mae Moffat

Dear Lucy,

Thank you for the letter. I'm keeping it in my secret box. Nobody ever sent me a letter before. My mom's doing better, but we both still get pretty sad sometimes. Cleveland isn't so bad. I'm going to a new school and the kids are nicer than at my last school. Cleveland's on Lake Erie and some of the kids at my school have sailboats. They belong to a sailing club, kind of like the Cove Fleet. Their boats aren't prams, I asked them. But one boy said he'd take me for a ride. Just like you guys did.

Maybe I'll get to learn to sail after all.

Yours truly,
Henry Addison

P.S. Thanks for being my friend. Tell Jack.

EPILOGUE

WEEKS LATER THE WATER WAS PUMPED OUT *of the* Noronic *and she floated once more. But she could not be salvaged. The steel of her superstructure was twisted into grotesque forms and not a sliver of wood remained. The three upper decks had been cut away to remove the dead. Her captain's licence had been taken away and her crew scattered. The ashes of the great lady had blown away on the wind. She was a death ship.*

The only part of the Noronic *left intact was her famous whistle. Canada Steamship Lines offered the whistle to all of its captains. Nobody wanted it. It was cursed.*

A month after the disaster the tug Rival *fixed a line to the dead Queen and hauled her out of Toronto Harbour. Seven* Noronic *officers stood at attention on the bow, hats removed in mourning, as she was towed across the lake to the scrapyards in Hamilton. Nothing was said; no orders were issued.*

The Queen was a ghost ship. Born in a storm, she died in a fire, a captain's worst nightmare. The SS Noronic *was* truly cursed.

AUTHOR'S NOTE

THE QUESTION I AM MOST OFTEN ASKED by readers is "How much of the story is true?"

Life on Ward's Island in the 1940s was very similar to Jack's life. Many islanders shared their memories of that time with me, and I am grateful to them for their stories. The Cove Fleet, the camp-outs on Snake Island, bicycle polo and Supervision were all a part of island life. Jack, though, comes from my imagination, as do the other members of the crew and their families. In this book I have used some names that will be familiar to past and present islanders, but the characters attached to the names are fictional.

One thing that does come straight from history, however, is Jack's "trusty steed." It originally belonged to George Stein who was indeed a very skillful cyclist.

My personal memories of Ward's Island date back many years. Although my family had sold their island cottage by the time I was born, they were still islanders at heart. Each year our whole family would return on Gala Day, the island's summer celebration, to catch up with old friends and "mess about with boats."

THE NORONIC

The tragic fire on the *SS Noronic* is, unfortunately, true. The death toll stands at 118, and all of those who died were passengers, most of them American. Every member of the crew, including the captain, escaped. Ross Leitch is a real character, and did use his water taxi to pull at least fifty people from the harbour waters on the night of the disaster.

To find out the details of that night I talked to eye-witnesses, read newspaper articles and books and studied the official disaster report. Many questions may have come to mind as you were reading about the fire. Why didn't the firehose work? Why didn't the crew wake the passengers? Why was no one in the wheelhouse where the alarm bell was? Why was there only one gangplank? How did all the crew escape when so many passengers died? These are all very good questions.

There was a government inquiry after the disaster. The same questions were asked. The inquiry found that the firefighting equipment was in working order but that there wasn't enough of it. It also determined that the terrible loss of life was in part the result of poor crew training. Neither the *Noronic*'s owners nor the captain had prepared the crew to deal with a fire. The consequences of that poor training were twofold: the owners paid two million dollars to the victims and their families and the captain lost his licence for one year. He never went back on a laker.

The *Noronic* disaster changed history in two ways. Firstly, Canada dramatically changed the fire safety regulations for the Great Lakes cruise boats, adding many safety features. Unfortunately, the safety features were so expensive that boat owners believed they couldn't afford them, and so many boats were taken out of service. The cruises, so popular for forty years, were largely over.

Secondly, the extreme heat of the fire all but incinerated the victims. In order to make identifications, several brand new techniques in forensics were invented. Those techniques are still in use today.

A plaque commemorating the *Noronic* can be found in Harbour Square Park, next to the Toronto Ferry Docks. The actual site of Pier Nine is now the lobby of the Harbour Castle Westin Hotel.

The Sabot Pram

The Sabot Pram originated in Scandinavia as a yacht tender. Made completely of wood, it was a useful but very heavy boat. When plywood was invented, a New

Yorker named Charles G. MacGregor created a set of plans for the pram using the lighter, cheaper material. The plans were published in a magazine called *The Rudder* in March 1942.

Jack Clapp, my grandfather, found the plans and arranged to have the first three prams built in the basement of his shoe shop for himself and his two sons, Donnie and Dougie. The two boys had already taught themselves to sail by "borrowing" their father's rowboat and using a canvas deck chair as a makeshift sail. The first pram built was called *Frosty Friday*.

The boats caught on, and the Ward's Island Cove Fleet was born. The Cove Fleet was the first to use this little dinghy as a racing boat, and Jack Clapp fielded requests from many parts of the world about his rigging changes, size alterations and one-design racing organization. Although the Cove Fleet on Ward's Island is no more, large fleets still exist in Florida and California. And in Australia, the Sabot Pram is the training boat of choice for all junior yachtsmen under the auspices of the Australian National Sabot Council. This is, in part, thanks to three boats built in the basement of a Toronto shoe shop.

Interestingly, all of the above areas claim to have been the first to sail Sabot Prams as one-design raceboats. But to my knowledge, the Cove Fleet predates all of them.

George Formby and his Ukulele

George Formby was one of the most popular stars of the 1940s. In fact, in 1941 he was named the world's fifth-biggest star, beating out even Bing Crosby and Bette Davis in popularity. When he died, over 150,000 people attended his funeral.

Formby appeared in twenty-one hit films, cut over 230 records, and entertained three million troops during World War Two. British by birth, he was extremely popular in Canada, Australia, South Africa and New Zealand, but never performed in the United States. At the height of his popularity, Formby was earning the equivalent of 8.6 million Canadian dollars a year.

His music was very popular on Ward's Island in 1949. Many of the boys had ukuleles, and they listened to records over and over in order to pick out Formby's chords. Then they created a songbook, drawing by hand all the chord boxes and laboriously typing the lyrics.

Whenever they learned a new song, the boys would take their ukes to the Ward's Island beach to impress the girls. And it always worked. George Formby had made sure that the ukulele was the hottest instrument around.

Songs of the Era

Many of the songs mentioned in the book are traditional summer camp songs. "The Titanic" song is sometimes called "Husbands and Wives" and sometimes "When the Great Ship Went Down." The *Titanic* sunk in 1912. Legend suggests that versions of this song began to appear in the southern United States within seven days of the disaster. Nearly one hundred years later, it is still being sung around campfires every summer.

"Junior Birdsman" is also a camp song. It has a lot of silly actions that go with the words. When I was a girl we would sing it over and over, faster and faster, until the words tangled in our mouths.

"Leaning on a Lamppost" was probably George Formby's most famous song. It has been rerecorded by numerous groups since Formby first sang it in 1937. The lyrics were written by Noel Gay.

Fun Facts About the Toronto Islands:

Nineteen-year-old Babe Ruth hit his first home run as a professional ballplayer at the Hanlan's Point Stadium, which held 10,000 people.

The Royal Norwegian Air Force used the Island Airport as their training base during World War Two.

The first residents of Ward's Island lived in tents. Gradually, the tents were replaced by wooden cottages.

Many famous Canadians have ties to the Toronto Islands:

- Ned Hanlan was born in 1855 and lived most of his life at Hanlan's Point. He was famous throughout Canada, Europe, the United States and Australia as a world champion rower. He is credited with introducing the sliding seat in racing skulls, and is well known for being so far ahead in his races that he could slow down to throw kisses to the girls before he finished – and still come in first.
- Paul Henderson, Olympic sailor (thanks to the Cove Fleet) and past president of the International Sailing Federation, lived on Ward's Island.
- Peter Gzowski, beloved Canadian broadcaster, had a Ward's Island home. He was president of the Ward's Island Association in 1969 and sailed a Sabot Pram in the resurrected Cove Fleet in 1971.
- Sam McBride, two-time Mayor of Toronto, was one of the first tenters on Ward's Island.
- Sir John A. MacDonald regularly attended boating events on the Toronto Islands.
- Jack McClelland, of McClelland and Stewart Ltd. Publishers, spent his childhood summers on the Toronto Islands.

FUTURE OF THE ISLAND:

The island lifestyle has changed little in the sixty years since this story took place. Everyone still uses a bicycle for transportation. Few prams are left, but other sailboats dot the waters. Children play outside all day long, and all the neighbours still know one another.

But keeping this lifestyle has been an ongoing fight for the island community, situated just ten minutes away from the largest city in Canada. There is great pressure on the land. Some people want the islands to be a public park. Some people want to build condominiums. So for protection, the Toronto Islands have been put into a Community Trust to manage the land and buildings for both the islanders and the general public. There are about seven hundred residents who still live on Ward's and Algonquin Islands.

Today, most of the Toronto Islands are public parks. Thousands of people ride the ferry boats across the harbour to enjoy swimming in the lake, a visit to the amusement park on Centre Island or a leisurely bicycle ride along the Boardwalk. If you go, make sure you visit Ward's Island too. It is a reminder of a simpler time. I hope the islanders will be able to stay there forever. A visit to their little piece of the world makes my heart sing.

ACKNOWLEDGEMENTS

The stories of life on Ward's Island have always been near and dear to my heart. My sincere thanks to all of the Ward's Islanders, past and present, who shared their stories, their photographs and their memories with me: most particularly my father, Doug Clapp, who will always be an islander at heart.

I would also like to thank Donna Mae (Peirce) and Don Clapp, whose memories provided depth and balance; Albert Fulton, Island archivist, whose help with the research and final editing was much appreciated; the Van Camp family: John, Dawn, Barry and Frances; Les Lye; Ken Lye; Pat (Garnett) Rea; Maud (Groat) Stevenson; Barry Barnett; Whitney Webster — without all of you, this book would not have been possible.

As always, I want to thank my editor, Barbara Sapergia. Our conversations make me laugh, and think.

And heartfelt thanks to my husband Dale, who makes all things possible.

ABOUT THE AUTHOR

PENNY DRAPER LEARNED TO SAIL off the shores of Ward's Island when she was ten. Her father took her out in a fourteen-foot sailboat and tipped it over on purpose, dumping her into Lake Ontario. "The first lesson," he said, "is not to be afraid of falling into the water." She learned fast. It was better than getting wet.

This is Draper's second novel for young adults. Her first, *Terror at Turtle Mountain*, was short-listed for the Silver Birch Award and the Diamond Willow Award.

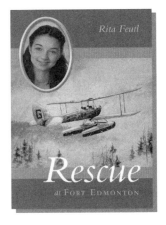 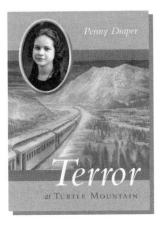

Adventures at Sea!

Look for another exciting Coteau Books for Kids series, *Ghost Voyages,* by award-winning author, Cora Taylor.

Ghost Voyages
Cora Taylor
978-1-55050-197-1
$6.95CAD/$5.95USD

Ghost Voyages II:
The Matthew
Cora Taylor
978-1-55050-198-8
$6.95CAD/$5.95USD

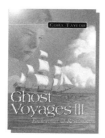

Ghost Voyages III: Endeavour & Resolution
Cora Taylor
978-1-55050-305-0
$7.95CAD/$6.95USD

Amazing Stories • Amazing Kids